HATTIE WADE

Rebounds & Roses

First edition

ISBN: 979-8-9912875-2-4

*This book was professionally typeset on Reedsy.
Find out more at reedsy.com*

To Little Caesar, Lilah, Bobbles, Aureole, Tsetse and Shifty, Beadie, and Jack.
Your owner is the best. Never take her for granted.

Contents

Acknowledgments

This book was inspired by two special people in my life. They know who they are. A BIG thanks to them for letting me write about bits and pieces of their lives.

In the book, Rosie's best friend is named Sara. Her name is Sara in honor of all the special Sara(h)'s I have in my life. Particularly, my high school Sara/Sarah's. There were three. I couldn't have done high school without them.

A big thanks to my College Basketball playing neighbors, for letting me name drop them into the book.

To my Betas; SB, HN, AL, TL, RM, and CS. Thanks so much you guys!!

To my lovely editor, Rachel at Get Proofed LLC. I couldn't do this without you.

Thank you Mo, for listening to my brainstorming continuously and always praying for me.

Thank you to all my readers. All your support means the world. It allows me to continue to write! Thanks so much.

All Glory Goes To God!
   Hattie Wade

(Acknowledgments section is not professionally edited.)

Chapter 1

"Hi there, Mr. Bass, my name is Rosalie St. Clair, and I would like to have one minute of your time. I believe you are on the Board of Research at the university. Well, I wanted to talk to you about all my compelling research I've done on the species called Lymantria dispar, aka the—"

Click.

Why doesn't anyone ever take me seriously? One would think with a big word like Lymantria dispar, people would be on the edge of their seats, dying to know what that is. But that is my fifth. *Fifth. Rejection. This. Week.* Fourteenth rejection this month.

"It's not my week," I sigh as I drive my chopsticks into my chow mein. Because of my track record, I had a feeling tonight would not go in my favor. So, I grabbed an extra fortune cookie at the Chinese restaurant. I thought perhaps one of them could change my fate. It was worth a shot. Who am I kidding? That was a shot in the dark, and I'm no basketball player. So instead, now they are my pity cookies.

1

"I'm simply trying to look out for the little guys. Don't give me that stare, Shifty, I'm not only researching the not-so-great crop-eating moths, but I'm also researching the beneficial-to-our-environment moths, and don't you think I am fibbing to you. You know I love you and your friends." I lovingly eye my tarantula named Shifty and all her surrounding friends. I plop down onto my pleather couch and text my best friend.

Sara has been my best friend since elementary school. After high school, the majority of our friend group went off, out of state for school. But Sara and I remained here. I attended the University of Illinois for both my undergraduate zoology degree and my graduate level entomology degree. Sara became a hairdresser. And a pretty good one at that—just ask my dead ends—oh wait, you can't! Ha! Sara tells me I have the sense of humor of a middle-aged dad. I don't see the problem, although she insists I will never get a man like that.

Though doesn't she know? I'm not trying to land a man, simply a research grant.

However, both of those tasks are proving to be rather impossible indeed.

A few loud knocks rattle my door, followed by two quiet knocks, and I shout, "Come in!" While my answer is a bit gutsy—it could be anyone—only Sara knocks that way. We have a secret friendship knock. My brother, Ryder, as soon as he discovered this, had a cow. He gets onto me all the time about being safer. He's a caring older brother, and I suppose soon I should listen to him.

Tonight is not one of those times.

"Rosalie St. Clair, the single best entomologist I have ever met, please tell me you have good news about your moths!" She flings a plastic sack onto my couch and sets two boba teas on my coffee table.

"First off, I am the only entomologist you know, and second, no such luck. No one cares about the little guys other than me, apparently." I sigh, eyes widening at the beautiful view of my mango passion fruit boba tea.

"Did they at least let you explain what Lymantria dispar is?" she asks, opening the plastic bag and whipping out two gluten-free stroopwafels. She's gluten free. I feel bad for her but will eat any gluten-free snacks she brings over to offer her condolences.

"No, he hung up on me." I shrug.

"If we had a dollar for every time that's happened to you, I think you'd have enough money to fund your research project," she teases me.

"Ouch, low blow, Sara." I poke her shoulder with my chopstick as she sits down next to me and grabs the remote.

"I wasn't talking about your professional life, Rosie." Sara clicks power on the remote control and leans back into the couch, beginning to channel surf.

"That doesn't make it any better," I scoff, glancing at her.

"Although, you are right. Rejection is kind of my word of the year—or … *eh*, years." I consider this last year and the past string of years, and I come to the same conclusion. *Rejection is my word*.

How does one change that? I don't want my fate to be "the girl who is rejected." I want to be accepted and heard.

Understood, and not just tolerated.

I'm interrupted from my train of thought when Sara spews her boba out of her mouth. "Is that Washington on tv?"

Washington. That is Clarke Washington. He went to high school with us, in the grade above. He's Ryder's best friend—

well, ex-best friend. *Drama.*

"Of course he's on tv. Chicago is playing tonight." I roll my eyes and stuff my mouth full of greasy goodness. Sara looks over at me and cringes. Her cringe changes into a sly smile, and my stomach does a flip.

"Remember when I first asked you 'who's that?'" She grins.

Oh boy. I flashback to the gym my freshman year of high school. When I think back on memories, I remember them so vividly I can smell them and hear music. Is that normal? Anyways, in this flashback, I smell gym shoes and the all-too-common stench of basketballs. And I hear … I hear—oh no, it's going to get stuck in my head now— "Basketball" by Bow Wow. My nostrils flare as I'm sucked into the memory: I'm sitting up on the bleachers with Sara. She points to the door and asks, "Is he new?" My eyes go from my skinny jeans to the gym door. In walks, in almost a montage, my brother, Ryder St. Clair, and his best friends Kevin Yates, Jaxon Murray, Sawyer Lawrence, and Brock Keller. Also, yeah, a new kid. They're only sophomores, but they are good enough to be on the varsity basketball team. They are the ones to watch. That is, *if you watch.*

I look over at her as I reach for the plastic sack and pull out my stroopwafel. "Technically, you asked if he was new, not who is that." I smirk at her.

"So you do remember! How about that time when you …," she continues.

"Oh, don't you even say it, S. You know you were the one who gave him that Valentine sophomore year. You stuck it in his locker but didn't put your name on it, and Ryder accused me of putting it in there!" I wave my finger in the air.

"Oh yes, I remember Ryder delivering a stellar rejection

4

speech to you in the bus line and telling you that his friends were off-limits." She laughs.

"Yeah, little did he know, I couldn't care less about his friends. All I cared about was my bugs." I shrug and take a bite of the stroopwafel.

"And books," Sara adds.

"And books." I hold up my stroopwafel to tap it against her boba tea.

"Cheers," we both say.

"If only times were easier, like in high school," Sara says as she sucks up a tapioca pearl.

I look at her like she's lost her mind. High school? Easy?

"How was high school easier than our current fates?" I probe her.

"Well now, we're both single, hardworking, and exhausted adults. I'm gluten free." She sighs.

"I knew it, it's about gluten. Hey, that would rain on anyone's parade." I nod.

"Rosie, I'm serious. Just think of how carefree high school was," Sara says dreamily.

"I'd rather not." Apparently, we share completely different memories of high school. It's not like it was awful, but I was a ghost. My family was *the* basketball family. My brother, Ryder, and sister, Roxy, both played super competitively. And I did not. 'Nuff said. At least for right now.

To cut Sara off about the glory days, I decide to dig into my self-deprecating humor. "Remember that next year's Valentine's Day," I say, instigating her.

"Oh my gosh," she chuckles, "Parker O'Brien, poor guy."

"Yeah, good ole Parker O'Brien. I think he's a real estate agent in New Jersey now," I state.

"Maybe if you hadn't put that snakeskin in the envelope, it would've gone better," she lectures me.

"Pssh. It was cool. I wanted to give my crush something cool," I defend myself.

"Except you're the only one who thinks that's cool and not gross." She shakes her head at me and furrows her brow.

"Fair. Well, I never wanted to move to New Jersey anyway." I shake my head and reach for my boba tea.

Sara tosses a throw pillow at me, and I block it. We laugh over the misfortunes of my love life.

Looking back at the tv and watching Clarke Washington go up for a layup, I think of the pain he caused my brother and my family. So, sure, thinking about the past can be fun, but I for one am thankful that it is just that—*the past.*

Chapter 2

⚜

I thought that my two degrees that cost me about a hundred thousand dollars in student loan debt would have gotten me farther by now. Dad says if I would just let the research go and settle down in a steady job I could find more success. I love my dad, but he doesn't understand me. He never has. I am passionate about this research project. It is cutting-edge. We are on the cusp of discovering more about the migratory patterns and behaviors of spongy moths. This research could play a role in protecting crops and forests from defoliation, and therefore, in turn, farms and possibly farming families. It is crazy to think that such a small moth could bring such destruction. My research project directly plays into agricultural pest management. This could be groundbreaking. There is a group of us at the university who are extremely passionate in this area. When we presented it before the leadership, they informed us we would each have to find our own way of funding the project. Which was a royal pain in the butt.

I suppose you could say I am just as much of a ghost now as I was in high school. There are a select few of us out there who really care about insects. Most of the time, I am considered a freak, even by my own family. Just because I have different interests doesn't make me a freak. My senior class dubbed me "the girl with the pretty face who is friends with spiders." That made the guys in the film club reach out and ask me how I felt about playing Spiderwoman in their new upcoming play. They claimed it was a breakout from gender norms. Yeah, no, I turned them down very quickly.

That's fine, no one had to understand. I've been doing this thing—my life—on my own for quite some time now. I've managed to collect a few friends along the way who share my passion for bugs and critters. I have Sara in my corner, and I have my little personal zoo within my apartment. That's all I need. I'm happy.

As I wait to get a grant, I have to have some steady flow of income, so I have gone back to my trusty animal control job. I have gone back to this job back and forth over the years. I always have adventures on this job. Whether it's snake calls, stray dogs and cats wandering subdivisions, or the occasional skunk in the garage. It's always a good time.

As I'm getting ready for my shift, I tighten the laces on my boots and slip my platinum blonde hair into the navy ballcap. I know what you are thinking: platinum blonde hair on this girl? Well, my best friend is a hairdresser, after all. I let her experiment on me. For better or worse.

Ring, ring.

"Hello?" I hold my phone to my ear.

"Rosie, we can't see you, honey!" my mom says rather loudly. I cringe. Huh?

I hold my phone out in front of me. *Ah shoot, a video call. And the whole gang is here. Oh my.*

What did I accidentally get myself into?

"We need to have a family meeting, you guys. Rosie, honey, your face looks like you did not check your email this week." My grandma sits in front of their tablet with a clipboard in her hand. My grandpa just sits next to her, looking happy to be alive.

"It is only Tuesday, Grandma," I mutter but smile with my teeth. I know Grandma likes to see my teeth.

"Okay, kids, listen up," my mom begins. The screen switches between all of our faces. Ryder is in his office in Minneapolis, Roxy is presumably sitting in her dorm room in Virginia, and Grandma and Grandpa are at their home in Naperville. Mom and Dad are at theirs too, also in Naperville. I press my finger to the screen and pause the screen on my grandparents for a moment. There are men carrying cardboard boxes back and forth in the background. Huh.

"Just say it, Sharon," my dad urges my mom to go on.

"Grandma and Grandpa are selling Love in Bloom," she says abruptly.

My heart drops to my stomach, and I feel as if I might puke or pass out. Thank God I'm not driving yet.

"What?!" I exclaim at the same time Roxy and Ryder say, "Okay."

"No, not okay, Grandma! Gramps! You can't sell Love in Bloom! It's iconic," I plead.

"Sorry, hun, we have to move into assisted living, and we need the money."

"Hire on some more help. It's peak season; you'll be rolling in the dough! You know how much this state loves your garden!

9

People travel all over for their special picture underneath the rose arch. It's a Chicago staple!" I plead.

"Rolling in the dough …?" Dad questions my word choice, and I hear Ryder snicker.

"Grandma, please, don't sell the garden. It's too special to everyone." *To me,* I want to say. *It's special to me.*

"We haven't marketed the rose garden like that in years, Rosie," Grandma explains solemnly.

"You still have loyal customers, don't you? You told me Marge takes a yearly photo under the rose arch! Everyone believes it brings good marital bliss, since you and grandpa got engaged under the arch and are still going strong!" I try to think of anything I can.

"Marge died last year, honey." Well, there goes that angle.

"Our generation is aging out, and we are not up with the hipness of culture. We are losing money," Grandma says.

I'm losing this battle. I can feel it. This rose garden is so special to me. I spent every summer as a child with my grandparents when Roxy and Ryder had special travel basketball camps and pre-season scrimmages. I have so many lovely memories of reading books in the garden, feeling a bit like Alice in Wonderland. Learning about pests and how to control them. Watering the roses through the hot and humid summers. I loved watching the giddy couples line up for their photo under the rose arch. So many people were in love, all around. It never made me sick to my stomach either, just left me feeling hopeful. While I do look at my love life differently now, if they sell this garden, that's it. The love ship has sunk; there really is no hope for me. *The bug lady.*

"Oh, I have a pleasant suggestion," Dad begins, and I instantly feel the hair on my neck stand up.

"You are still in town, Rosie, and your butterfly studies include flowers, right? You could get the rose garden hype going again for this younger generation, and if it makes enough for Grandma and Grandpa, we can keep the garden in the family, and if it doesn't fare well, well then they can sell it."

I swear my chin has dropped to my feet. *Um. What? Rewind. Sorry. What?*

"I … Uh …" I stumble, and Roxy laughs in the background. I frown at the camera. "What is it, Rox?"

"Sorry, sorry, Dad just said that you can get the hype going again for the younger generation, but what do you know of it? You're in your thirties," she howls.

I blink, unimpressed by my little sister. She's right though. But I am desperate to keep this in the family. It's the only thing in my family that feels like mine. I don't want to let it go.

"You could help her, Roxy," Mom interjects.

"Hey, no, Roxy has to focus on this next season coming up," my dad says.

I roll my eyes.

"Right, Dad. Plus, I have eighteen hours this semester." She shakes her head. "Sorry."

She's not sorry.

"Well, we are going to move forward with the sale—" Grandma starts, and before I know what my mouth is doing, noise is blubbering out.

"No, no, don't sell it. I'll do it. I'll get it fixed up and running again. I'll get the business booming again. It will be good. People just need to remember what Love in Bloom was," I say and glance at my watch. I need to go.

"Are you sure, honey?" my grandma questions me.

"I'm positive. I'll take it."

Dad claps his hands together, and his face lights up. "Excellent! There ya go, Rose! Hey, Rosie's Roses! Just in case you need a new brand name."

Okay, now I feel sick.

Absolutely. Not. That.

Grandma's face matches mine, very disapproving, and thank God for that.

"Look, I have to get to work, but—" I start.

"Give them your two weeks!! My baby is entering the business world! She's settling down! Watch out, world!" Dad jumps up from the couch and elbows my mom, smiling. She fakes a smile for him. But I think she's like me; she's nervous.

But I guess … I guess I'll do it afraid.

Chapter 3

I pull my old black Mazda into the gravel parking lot of Love in Bloom. I park and step out, taking in the sight around me. There is a cute little check-in area with a chalkboard. I picture the sweet font that used to live on that board, but now it's all wiped away. A few wooden planks hang off the welcome bridge—yikes, I need to get that fixed as soon as possible. I peek beyond the welcome bridge into the garden; the roses are growing just as they should. That's a blessing. I bet Renee and Jose have still been tending to it. What gems. It would be much harder if it was overrun with weeds. There would be no way I could open it to the public until next year. But I don't know, maybe I could plan for a grand reopening? It's too late for the summer season, as it's already the beginning of September. But maybe I could do one big reopening, and then stay open until mid-October? Then, next year, go all in! Did I just bite off way more than I can chew?

I carefully cross the bridge into the garden and peek around the blush pink roses. There in front of my eyes is a rickety, outdated version of the most beautiful rose arch you could imagine. It sits right to the side of the pink barn; the barn simply houses the tools it takes to take care of the garden. But maybe I could change that. Or, I don't know, maybe bring in a food truck? People like food, right? These are big plans for one little me. I can't believe my family was so quick to toss this place aside. Yet again, my siblings were rarely here, and when they were, they couldn't care less for the scenery.

The hype of the rose garden started in 1953. My grand-parents have the most adorable love story. They are high school sweethearts, and my grandpa has a purple heart from the Korean war. Yes, they check off many of the major romance plots and tropes. High school sweethearts, check. Friends to lovers, check. Soldier writing letters home, check.

Grandpa Bill left for war before he could ask Grandma Irene to marry him. Grandma stayed behind, and her and her friends started working on this rose garden on the back of her dad's land. Grandma Irene and Grandpa Bill wrote letters back and forth and missed each other terribly. When Grandpa came home injured from war, they didn't know if he would make it. When he did, the first place Grandma brought him was the rose garden. She tells the story way better than me. He was in a wheelchair from his injury but looked at all Grandma Irene had done while he was gone, and he said it gave him hope for their future together. After the president recognized Grandpa for his purple heart, Grandpa dropped a secret in the photographer's ear. He told him of his plan to propose to Grandma under the rose arch, at the coolest new place to purchase or simply ponder roses.

It was also significant because he would be getting out of his wheelchair for it, after countless months of rehab. While my grandpa doubted the man would show, the prestigious photographer did indeed show up to the garden and took the photo of Grandpa proposing. That picture would wind up on the front page of the Chicago Tribune that summer of 1953. It drew a very large crowd. I think my grandpa still has that newspaper clipping. I think it's framed. I need to get my hands on that before it is boxed up. There may be something in there that gives me an idea for marketing. Well, that photographer didn't only take the picture, he also penned up a beautiful caption, and then a journalist took the rest of the credit.

Crowds would appear, begging to have their photos taken under the rose arch. Grandpa and Grandma ended up hiring a photographer. People would come back, year after year. And maybe some of that was thanks to the ten-year check-ins by that original photographer. The photographer always got their ten-year check-ins printed in the paper. The newspaper journalist would ask them different questions every year about love and its longevity. People believed they would have good luck in their relationships if they were able to come just once and see this place. But once people came, more often than not, they became repeat attendees.

But the times changed, and as social media took over and people stopped reading their newspapers, Love in Bloom faded out. Surely I can figure something out. It will take social media, I'm sure. I want to keep the garden's namesake, and I want it to pay homage to the original story. I just don't know how to put all of this together.

Oh, what did I get myself into?

"Are you still dating Peter? Just his presence here could attract a new crowd," Grandma says from behind me. I startle.

"Yeah, I am definitely not dating that jerk anymore," I say, crossing my arms around my chest.

What she doesn't have to know is that he broke up with me. Rejection #347, but who is keeping count? I feel like I'm a teen again, watching a show, and there are cheerleaders around me chanting, "R-E-J-E-C-T-I-O-N!" but it's brought on by my grandma Irene.

"I'm afraid to say it, but your singlehood is not going to help your case," she observes.

Thanks, Granny.

But she's right—my solo life is not going to be the marketing I need. How can I convince others to come here and have luck in their love life if I am indeed single? I need to plan with Sara. She is a hairdresser by day and an occasional wedding coordinator (for the right fee) by night. Surely she can throw more love on this place than me. We need to bring the crowd back. I need to bring the crowd back, I gulp. Whether I like it or not, this is now my special project, because the money from this will not only keep the garden in the family, but it will fund my grandparents' stint in assisted living and maybe even my research.

Again, what did I get myself into?

Chapter 4

"Hey, girl, you don't look so hot. Hard day?" Sara asks me as I fling my black purse onto the bar.

"Ugh, like you couldn't imagine." I huff and puff my platinum blonde hair out of my face.

"Another rejection?" Sara seems to regret asking that as soon as the words leave her mouth. She cringes at my annoyed expression.

"Okay, well enough of that. Which drinks are we trying tonight? Open a menu. Close eyes. And ..." We both hold menus in front of us, extend our pointer fingers, and hover over the drink options with our eyes shut.

"Go!" Sara exclaims.

As our fingers fly down, Sara quickly looks at my choice. "Oh man, Rosie, this really isn't your day. You literally got chocolate milk on the children's menu. How!" I scoff and facepalm myself.

"Can I please break our tradition and just get a rum and coke?" I beg her.

"Rosalie St. Clair! No, this has been our tradition forever. You get what you get," Sara begins.

"And you don't throw a fit, yeah, yeah I remember." I fold my arms and pout.

"You are acting three instead of thirty-one." Sara glances at me.

"I feel like I'm three, ordering a glass of chocolate milk at a bar. What are you getting, S?" I look over at her finger pressed against her menu.

"Sangria? Ugh, lucky." I roll my eyes at my best friend.

"Are you coming with me on Saturday so you can get a fresh haircut for fall?" Sara asks as she flags down the bartender.

"It will depend on how much research …," I begin before I get distracted by Sara's jaw, which has gone ajar while watching the tv above us, and then her head looks to our right.

"Is that Washington?" Sara says. This feels like déjà vu.

"Sara, yes, we have established that Washington does indeed play basketball professionally," I explain to her.

"No," she nudges me, "*there.* Don't look too hard."

I spin on my barstool and look towards the front door.

"What is he doing back here … He hasn't been back here since that night," I say, recounting a tough memory.

"What night?" Sara asks.

"Uh, erm, graduation night 2009," I say, still stunned to see him here, in the flesh.

"We graduated in 2010," Sara states, still one step behind my train of thought.

"Yep, I meant Ryder's graduation. Don't acknowledge him, Sara; turn around, unless you want to end up on social media later. No thanks." I swivel my chair back to the counter. I hear people fawning over him. Ugh.

18

"So we're taking the 'we don't recognize him' road?" she asks, nodding to the bartender, who hands her the sangria.

"Correct." I nod confidently and throw back my chocolate milk.

"Oh gosh, Rosie, don't look, he is sitting down right next to you." She gestures just to my left.

"Stop. You are joking," I tease her.

But then I hear his deep voice behind me. I freeze.

Abort. Abort. Abort. Mission.

What mission?!

As Sara silently encourages me to say something, I sit there, my back to Washington, staring at poor Sara like a deer in the headlights.

He hasn't noticed us yet, thank God.

Sara goes to stand, and I stare her down, my eyebrows raise, as if to say, "WHAT ARE YOU DOING?"

She waves off my concern. That could only mean one thing.

Oh, no.

I take one more quick sip of my chocolate milk and plan to make a beeline toward the door.

As Sara moves to my side, I stand to run out. I pull on the strap of my black bag, and that is when all chaos ensues.

My bag hits my chocolate milk, which spills, e v e r y w h e r e …

People gasp, and all the people in about a five-mile radius jump up from their barstools. Okay, that is an exaggeration, but it sure feels that way.

My bag strap gets caught on the back of my barstool, and I just want to crawl in a hole and die because this whole ordeal has definitely got me spotted. Not only spotted, but I look up to phones. Lots of phones, capturing my distress. *Oh, brother.*

These twerps.

I yank and yank on the strap of my bag. I just need to leave, to get away from this bar. Gosh, this is the worst day ever. I put all I have into a final yank, and it sends me into a twirl. I watch my life flash before my eyes; I am going to slam my head into something. But, as my heart pounds in my chest, I'm suddenly caught up in a set of strong chocolate arms.

Double oh no.

"Rosalie?"

Washington caught me—of course he did.

I unravel myself from his arms and make a beeline towards the door. I'll come back later for my bag. I can't do this now.

I dig around my jeans pockets, and thank God, my keys are indeed in a pocket. As I open my driver's door, I climb in and get settled into the front seat. I need to go home. I need to just shake it off.

What was that, Rosie?

That was what happens when you have history with someone and haven't seen them in fifteen years. But that couldn't be it, could it? I mean, it's not like we ever dated. But he did mean a lot to my family, and then one day fifteen years ago, he left; he walked out of our lives without warning. And now what? Now he just gets to walk right back in? Nah.

I do some breathing exercises in the safety of my car, and my back pocket vibrates; it's a text from Sara.

"I'm assuming you are not coming back in? I'll be out in one second with your soaked purse. We don't have to talk right now. But we will later," the text reads.

Hooray.

But I understand. I don't get to act like that without an explanation to my best friend. Only problem is, I don't have an explanation.

As Sara walks out to my car, I roll my passenger side window down.

She hands me my bag and shrugs. "I'm gonna stay here for a bit and catch up." I blankly nod at her; my throat is dry.

She turns to walk back into the bar but stops to shout over her shoulder, "Oh, by the way, you've got a milk mustache!"

Oh. My. Gosh. Seriously?

Chapter 5

I t's the morning after my least finest hour. Sara sent me a meme of my face last night, and I can only pray it doesn't go viral because that's the last thing I need—bad press. I decided to single handedly take on the chore of repainting the check-in desk. I want it to match the pink hues of the barn. So it's me and my trusty paint brush out here today. It's a mild September day; I'm thankful for that, as I know this will take quite a bit of time. I can't wait for the fall weather to start in full swing.

About two hours into my painting, I'm really breaking into a sweat. I reach down the ladder for my water bottle but can't quite grab it.

I turn around, grumbling a bit to myself and climb down the ladder. As I turn around, I startle as I hear a familiar deep voice.

"Well if it isn't little Rosie St. Clair, now the sole owner of Love in Bloom Rose Garden? It's Rosie's rose garden." He moves over to me, reaching in to give me an awkward side hug. All five feet, seven inches of me peeks up at six-foot-seven basketball player, Clarke Washington.

"What are you doing here, Washington? I haven't seen you since graduation night. Then you ghosted everyone …" I guess I'm just going for it?

"You're chattier than last night," he says, smirking.

I glare at him.

"Last night was not my finest hour," I admit, chugging my ice water.

"You don't say?" He chuckles. "You seemed to be spooked. What spooked you?" He's talking smoothly, but it doesn't fool me.

"I don't know, Washington, maybe it was the ghost of graduation night 2009." I squint as the sun shines bright, and I'm trying to make eye contact with him. But he's so *very tall.*

"You're not gonna let that go, are you?" He gently kicks the gravel under his foot.

"Nobody has let it go," I state, placing my palm above my eyes to block out the sun.

"You didn't answer my question from earlier." I turn from him and start painting again. He sighs.

"Truth is, I'm needing a lawyer. Really, I need the best there is, and that's Ryder," he explains.

"Ry is not going to talk to you. He can't stand you." The words feel harsh as they leave my tongue, but it's the truth. I turn to look at him, my non-painting hand resting on my hip.

He gets a little closer to me and tilts his head. My stupid heart betrays me like this guy did to my brother. It raps quicker the closer he gets. It's just the height difference. All girls love a good height difference. Believe me, I read all about it in my books.

"What?" I shrug, glancing up at him, plenty annoyed.

"I was hoping for old times' sake you might reach out for me?" the jerk says.

"For old times' sake? Washington, I don't owe you anything," I scoff and shake my head in disbelief.

"I know that; of course I know that." He rakes his hand across his head. "It was worth a shot, but for real old times' sake, will you show me around this place …? There are so many memories from this rose garden with your grandma Irene." He smiles and looks around.

How does he remember? What does he remember? The fact is not lost on me that our arch nemesis has more positive memories of this place than my own brother.

"How are they?" he asks, glancing at the barn.

"In assisted living." I keep my answers short.

"Mmm … everyone is old now. I mean, even you, Rose Petal. You're what … pushing forty?" I can't see his face, but I know he's enjoying himself.

"Har, har. If that's the case, you're surely pushing fifty," I boldly spar back.

"I'm only two years older than you," he says back, taking the welcome bridge carefully. The thing is a hazard, I'm not going to lie. "White and pink this year? Something wrong with red?"

I snarl at him—him and his lame opinions.

He bends down to smell the roses, and I can't help but think of the quote, "Don't forget to stop and smell the roses." I smile. I want people to come; I want them to enjoy the roses. I might put that quote on the new chalkboard.

He walks a bit ahead of me, hands in his pockets. I can't see his face, and maybe that's what gives me this false sense of courage.

"You know, Grandma Irene was the only one who wasn't angry when you left. She figured you had a reason. Did you?" I ask curiously. I don't know if his answer would change anything. But if there's anyone here who owes something to someone, it's him.

"It was good to see you, Rose Petal." Classic. Typical. He completely ignores my question. I'm not sure what I was expecting.

We walk back to the welcome bridge, and he reaches out to touch me. My instinct is to dodge him, and so I do, but unfortunately, my brain doesn't register the danger just beyond me.

"Geez! Rosie!" He reaches out and grabs ahold of me, pulling me into his arms again.

"Why did you flinch away? Can't you just give me a hug like a normal person? Do you have to get yourself into danger at every turn?" My hands rest against his firm chest, and I linger in his arms for a moment.

Suddenly, I brush him off and gape at him.

"What? You're acting like I burned you." His voice is rough, laced with a twinge of hurt.

I shake my head. "We've never hugged before. I thought you were reaching to mess with my hair, like all you guys used to do when we were kids," I confess to him.

"Ahh, you were dodging the noogie." He smirks at me, and we both burst into a fit of laughter. It's a momentary truce.

"I was." A huge grin erupts on my face.

"Nope, rest assured, I was leaning in for a hug," he confirms to me.

I give him a side-eye, and he shrugs. "First time for every-thing?"

I shake my head and cross the hazardous bridge with him.

"You really should get that fixed. Get it up to code." He points to the bridge and then around the garden.

"That's the plan." I nod.

"I'll see you around, Rose Petal," he starts.

"You probably won't, *Washington*." I pop my hip to the side.

He smirks one last time, nods to me, and gets in his cab.

"Good riddance," I huff after he drives off. I have a lot of work to do.

Chapter 6

My fifty-second timer goes off on the microwave. I'll make my dinner once I feed my critters. I pull out the bowl of hot water and place it on my counter. Learning to open my freezer with my foot has earned me bragging rights when I'm with Sara. I dig at the back of my freezer. Shoot. I'm running out of mice. I make a mental note to get more next week. Lilah is my eleven-year-old albino corn snake. She eats two mice every two–three weeks. I snatch the last frozen rodent and drop it in the lukewarm water to thaw. She is going to love this feast. I grab a paper plate from my lower cabinet; this way, when she eats the mouse, she won't ingest her aspen shavings.

Next is feeding my colony of spider beetles. I skip to the pantry and dig a measuring spoon into their oats bag. Don't worry, I don't use these same oats for my oatmeal. Ha. Unlike what Sara says, I'm not gross. I've collectively named these guys Bobbles. They love their oats and also some dry dog food.

After that, I think that's it. I already fed Shifty, my tarantula, and her best friend, Little Caesar, my male two-year-old dune scorpion. He eats crickets. Their aquariums sit next to each other. If critters had their own special language (and who am I to say they don't), these two would be chatting it up all day while I'm out. I can't explain it. They just look like the best of friends. Sometimes they hang out near the glass, and I just imagine all the conversations they are having.

As I wash my hands after serving Lilah, something catches my eye on my tv. It's ... it's the rose garden? And ... me? And *Washington*?

Oh, no, no, no, no, *no*.

I rush over to the tv and sit on the coffee table, chewing my nails. This cannot be happening.

It's a photo of me in Washington's arms. How? When? Ah, when I was dodging the noogie. Stupid noogie. The photo shows my hands on his chest as I lingered. I shouldn't have lingered. What was I thinking? As I'm starting to berate myself, I scramble for the remote and turn up the volume on the gossip.

The newscaster reports, "Love in Bloom Rose Garden, a name and place forgotten. But folks, let me remind you of this place. It has helped many past generations believe in love, and I think it's time we discover it again. You ask why? Well, I mean, just look at Rosalie St. Clair, new owner and granddaughter of power couple Irene & Bill. Before coming into ownership of Love in Bloom, she was as single as a red solo cup. But it appears the garden may be working its magic again. Love in Bloom was *the* place to come if you wanted to fall in love. Legend says if you have your photo taken beneath the rose arch, it guarantees good luck in your love life for years to come. Just look at Bill and Irene, the original owners. Their love story is beautifully laid out on our latest @KCBTChicago Instagram post. Now, we're not saying you will definitely connect with a professional basketball player on your visit to the garden. But, if Love in Bloom has shown us anything over the years, it's that anything is possible. Love in Bloom is just out in the suburbs of Chicago, in Naperville, IL. You can check out the garden from July–October. Back to you, Heather."

I can't. My mouth can't form words. I … uh. My mind is split. Half of me wonders why they're talking about my nonexistent love life on tv, and the other part thinks this is genius. Tears gather in my eyes. I don't believe it. I couldn't have asked for better publicity. I take out my phone and open Instagram, seeking the #beautiful love story of my grandparents.

Wow. They dug up old newspaper clippings. The every-ten-year anniversaries, the original proposal, the backstory of their proposal, Grandpa's photo with the president. *Everything*. I couldn't have done this without … Well, truth be told, I did nothing but dodge a noogie from my brother's ex-best friend. Sigh.

I have an eerie feeling. I'm going to have to see him again, aren't I? And it's going to be extremely awkward, especially if he's seen this newscast. Oh brother. Oh. My. Gosh. *Brother*!! What if Ryder sees this? He will feel so betrayed and confused. I need to clear my head; I need a plan. It's too late to go to the garden tonight. I'll head out first thing in the morning.

***

As I pull up to Love in Bloom in the morning, I can barely find a parking spot. *Oh my goodness.* I'm so overwhelmed. Paparazzi and newscasters flow in closer to the front gate. The garden isn't even open yet! And I … I should have put on makeup. Ah! I consider turning around and leaving, but I can't. I'm stuck. More people are pulling in behind me. I haven't seen the parking lot this full since I was a teenager. I don't want to turn people away, but the rose arch isn't completed, and heck, I can't forget about the welcome bridge that got me into this beautiful mess in the first place!

I just observe from my car. I hear one reporter talking next to the main gate, "Maybe it is possible to find love. You saw the picture with your own eyes! The lonely owner snagged herself a professional basketball player! Love in Bloom is lucky again!"

I decide to get out of my car, and at first, I'm not sure if it's wise, as reporters flock to me, and paparazzi snap their photos. Further proving my loner status, I'm sporting gray sweatpants and a Cubs shirt.

One reporter yells out, "Cubs? Shouldn't you be wearing a Bulls shirt?" I look down and gulp. I give a half-hearted smile back to him.

Another yells, "Rosalie, Rosalie! Tell us about you and Clarke's budding romance!! Budding, get it?" The woman snickers. That question nearly throws me into a panic, but then thank God for the other reporter who shouts out a different question that I can answer.

"Ms. St. Clair! What can you tell us about Love in Bloom?" I approach this man instead to give my answer.

"Everything you heard on tv, about Love in Bloom and my grandparents is absolutely true! This garden is special in so many ways! So, singles out there and also couples, I encourage you to come on back! My grand reopening is September 22nd!" I announce. "Now, if you'll excuse me, I have work to do!" I smile and march past the media to unlock the gate. I slip past and lock it back behind me.

Yes! I have a feeling I'm going to get all the money I need for my research! And Grandma and Grandpa will make plenty as well! I walk away smiling. But then I hear one last question by a woman reporter, and like dominos, all the other reporters begin asking similar questions.

"When will Clarke make an appearance?"

"Will you two lovebirds be at the grand reopening?"

"When will we see you two together again?"

"We want to know all about your meet cute!!"

And then finally, "Come on down folks, September 22nd!"

My smile turns into a cringe. Looks like "Good Riddance," really just meant, "Talk to you in two days."

Although? How do I get in touch with him? I don't have his number. Oh my gosh. I can't believe I'm about to do this. I open his Instagram, @TheREALClarkeWash, take a deep breath, and slide into his DMs.

Chapter 7

As the sun sets, I peer around the last row of roses. Oh, thank heavens, they're gone. As I dust my hands on my sweatpants, I kick myself for wearing sweatpants on a warm day. Given, I wasn't supposed to be here all day. I wasn't planning on it. But the reporters wouldn't leave, and I chickened out. I didn't want to deal with them again. I knew what they would ask about, and I have no answers for them about *that*. About *us*. Eesh.

As I unlock the front gate, I exit and then pull it shut behind me to lock it once again. Surely no one will be trying to break in. The rose arch isn't even done yet, but one can never be too careful. As I turn around, I jump at the sight in front of me. A *very* tall jock, with *very* stylish sunglasses leaning against a *very* fancy car.

"What do you want, Washington?" I groan.

"It's Clarke, and you said we needed to talk, remember?" His voice, ever so smooth, reminds me that indeed, I did say that.

I nod, supposing he is right, we have to talk. But first, I dig in my purse to find my car keys.

"I saw some reels that suggested you had a lot of business today—way more than the other day." He locks his car and approaches me.

"You seem to think you had something to do with that …" I huff, frustrated. I can't find my keys in this black hole of a purse. He's making it hard to focus, and not for the reason the reporters think.

I walk back to the gate, frantically looking for my keys. He follows my lead and wanders over to the gate as well. *There*! On the welcome desk! Ah, how could I be so clumsy? To get the gate key but not my car key?

As I press the key back into the lock again, Washington leans his arm against the gate and whispers down to me, "I know I did."

I roll my eyes. "Well, ugh, yeah, fine, you probably did. Did you see the news? People are ridiculous. We literally hugged." I laugh, somewhat nervously.

"You and I both know you dodged a noogie." A teasing smile tugs at his lips.

"Yeah, well, I …" Nope, I got nothing. I sigh in defeat; what was the point of this talk again? Why did I initiate this?

"Let's pretend to date," he calls after me as I scoop up my keys from the welcome desk.

"What?!" His words stop me in my tracks.

"If the garden has been struggling, it seems this is the way to get you more business. I can show up the rest of this season, and then once for your opening next year. It will keep the momentum going," he explains, making it sound logical. I narrow my eyes at him, shaking my head. No, no … *no*. But then my mind betrays me when it thinks, *maybe*? Maybe he's

33

onto something.

"No, please, I'm not that desperate." I grunt, waving him off.

"Sara told me you're seeking a grant." His voice grows louder. "What if this place brought in enough money for your grandparents, profit, and your research? No more rejections." He shrugs. "I don't know about you, but that sounds pretty good to me."

"Grr … Sara Snow. I'm going to kick her butt. I didn't realize anyone from Naperville still talked to you," I spit out, once again sounding harsher than I intended.

"Well, she did at the bar the other night." He clicks his tongue. "Come on, Rose Petal, what do you say? It's just like getting to know an old friend again."

I don't buy it.

"Please, Washington, we were never friends. You were my brother's best friend." I look up at him as I lock the gate again, hopefully for the last time tonight.

"Well, fine, we'll get to know each other then." He reaches out for a fist bump.

"I'm pretty sure if you actually knew me, you'd run for the hills." I laugh knowingly.

"I knew you once." He towers in closer, tilting his head, studying me.

"If you say so." My throat goes dry as I look from him back down to my keys.

I slide my hair into a scrunchie. "I need to get back home."

"So does that mean we're on?" he asks me, watching me approach my car.

"What's in it for you?" I spin around to ask him, trying to figure him out.

He works his jaw before saying, "Maybe if we are close, your brother …"

"You'll get his legal advice? I don't want to betray my brother's trust like you did. Why should I help you?" I question him.

"Look around; it would mainly be for you," he urges. I look around; today was a big day. I blow a flyaway hair from my face.

"Fine, but if it doesn't work, it doesn't work," I state.

As we both approach my car, I stick out my hand to shake his, but he closes his arms around me instead.

"What the heck? Do we need to set some rules about touching?" I wriggle my nose as I'm squished against his chest.

"There is a paparazzi over there in that yellow cab, back of the parking lot. I'm just trying to look chummy," he says into my hair.

"Well, in that case …" I boldly slip my arms around his waist. He meets my boldness with his own. He gently cups my face with his palms and places a light kiss to my forehead.

"Okay, okay …," I whisper, twisting in his arms; my heart warms without permission.

"Don't talk to anyone," he whispers back to me.

"Oh, don't worry about that," I promise him.

"Good." He nods.

"Want to go on a day date tomorrow?" he asks as I open my driver's door. He holds onto the door as I step into my car.

"Tomorrow? Already?" I hesitate for a moment.

"Sure, why not?" He shrugs his shoulders.

"Ah, fine." I nod.

"Send me your address," he says.

"How about you just pick me up here?" I deny him.

"Suit yourself. Eleven a.m.?" he suggests.

"See ya, Washington." I nod and put my car in reverse.

"Clarke." He points his finger back at me as he proceeds to his red sports car.

What have I gotten myself into?

Chapter 8

I awake with a start and look at my nightstand. The clock shines red back at me: 3:15 a.m. I lay my hand on my chest to steady my breaths.

I had a dream, but no, it was more like a flashback.

I heard Washington crying.

I'd forgotten. Late that night, graduation night. My parents had thrown a large party for Ryder and his crew. I stayed for the burgers and cake—oh, and the slideshow. Who could forget the slideshow? But as the sun set and darkness was cast across the sky, I got excused to go to bed. And then?

Then I snuck out. I opened my window and let in the warm Illinois wind. It tossed my blonde waves into my face and called me out to join. My parents' house has a large backyard, with my most favorite tree at the back of the property. I climbed down the roof and maneuvered myself off the pergola. Then I broke into a sprint. As I reached my tree, I felt free. I climbed up as I did nearly every weekend.

About two hours went by, and I heard howling laughter from

the party and drinks clinking together. The St. Clairs were always known for their good parties, never my scene though. I'd go out there with a book and read in the light of the moon.

As hour three approached, I figured I should go back inside. It was nearly midnight. I closed my book and took some deep breaths. Breathing in that fresh night air.

The next thing I knew, I heard some soft sobs; the sound came closer and closer to me. I stayed still as a statue. Not fully understanding what was going on. I mean, I was only sixteen. But even now … I still don't understand what I witnessed.

Why didn't I ask Washington why he was crying that night?

I mean, besides the obvious—I was Ryder's little sister, and I just caught him crying. I figured he'd be embarrassed.

I thought he walked back to the party, so I climbed down my tree. My feet landed on the ground, and when I heard shuffling to my right, I realized my error.

"Sorry," I said, very lackluster.

I was about to go back to my room when Washington stood up and said, "Rosie, Rosie, wait …" I turned to him as he said my name. Clarke was always Ryder's most quiet friend. His request caught me off guard.

I waited, staring up at him, as he walked closer to me. He reached out his hands, slowly enveloping mine in his. I was so confused. He looked so conflicted, so sad, so *free*.

"Rosalie," he whispered to me, and my heart rate picked up. A boy had never held my hands. Who was I kidding? A boy had never looked at me so longingly while saying my name.

But I couldn't speak; I was frozen in time. My eyes looked between him and the moon. The breeze blew my blonde hair into my eyes. He reached out and moved my hair back, behind my ear. The way his hand brushed up against my cheek … He

38

was so gentle.

He leaned in a bit, and for a moment, I thought right then, right there, I might get my first ever kiss. But he stopped then, his left hand squeezed mine, and all that left his lips was, "Goodbye."

He nodded and walked off. He exited the gate and shut it behind him. He never looked back, and I never called after him. I figured he had a rough night. I didn't see his parents at the graduation, and that had to hurt a guy. I figured I'd talk to Sara about all of this, we'd flesh it out, study it, reexamine it again, stew on it a little more, and then finally I'd work up the guts (maybe) to talk to him.

But he was gone. He never came back. I was so worried at first. I thought something happened to him. But then we heard. He got picked up to play at Duke University. He left for North Carolina, and he didn't tell a soul.

If only I'd asked him why he was crying.

If only I'd asked him.

And as I look back over, my clock reads 3:45 a.m., and I know that's enough stewing for tonight.

Chapter 9

"Y ou're wearing that?" His car crawls up, and he talks through the open passenger window.

"Pssh, okay, what's wrong with my khaki overalls?" I flaunt them for a second and do a little twirl.

"Socks and sandals?" He cringes.

"Birkenstocks," I correct him.

"Rosie, we're going to be out and about in Chicago, with paparazzi probably following me around," he explains.

"Hopefully," I reply, giving him a sly smile. If we're doing this, the paparazzi *better* be following us. If not, what's the point?

"Well, don't you want to dress up?" he asks again, rubbing his brow.

"Ugh, you are gross." I close the passenger door once I get in, but I consider opening it and walking off.

"I just mean …," he tries to cycle back.

"Are you embarrassed to be seen with me like this? Not one of your typical A-lister celebrity girls?" I lecture him.

"I didn't say that."

"You implied it," I challenge him. "*Look*, I forgot to feed Lilah after I went to the store this morning, so you have to come over to my place for a second before we go on our date." I look over at him.

"Okay," he agrees.

"Basically, I'm giving you an out. You still have time to decide if you can't deal with me. If you can't, you and your grand plan can leave back for the city," I confidently declare.

"Deal with you? Rose Petal, you are acting like we didn't know each other growing up. You are my best friend's little sister." He drums his fingers on the steering wheel.

"*Ex-* best friend," I enunciate.

"Ah, yes, thanks for the reminder." He sounds a little more hurt than I was expecting.

"Well, come on then, Wash … *Clarke*," I continue on.

"Thank you." He nods.

"If I am expected to call you Clarke, you cannot continue to call me Rose Petal. I'm not your sister, I'm your … fake dating person," I say, not sounding as smooth as I originally intended.

"Fair enough, *Rosie*." He pulls up to a stop sign

"Now turn here." I point to the left entrance at my apartment complex.

He pulls up to my apartment, and as I walk up the steps, he follows me.

"What kind of dog do you have? Or is it a cat?" he asks, chuckling.

Oh boy, he's in for a surprise.

"What?" I act like I can't hear him and hold the door so he can enter. I stride to the kitchen to wash my hands, and he nonchalantly follows me.

When he spies *that* bowl on the counter, he nearly vomits.

41

"What is in this bowl?"

"An adult mouse. I left it out accidentally. Thank heavens I remembered before we left on our date. It wouldn't be good this evening, and then I'd have to throw out a perfectly good meal," I ramble on.

"What the …?!" He looks at me in horror.

"For *Lilah,*" I emphasize, confused at his expression. What a big baby.

He looks so confused. Then it hits me—*oh.*

"Lilah, my corn snake," I state.

"Your *corn snake*?!" he exclaims.

Ahh, there it is.

"The door is over there." I shoot him a look. He looks around. Plastic enclosures and aquariums line my living room wall, my creatures of all sizes, creeping and crawling. He moves to my couch and looks above at the large map of Illinois. Certain cities are circled. A large blown-up picture of a moth is pinned on it. He looks at me like I'm a freak, and part of me is kinda hoping this is it. I don't need someone else in my life looking at me like that.

"What … is …" He looks around in awe.

"You know I'm an entomologist, right?"

"Is that some kind of …," he begins.

I glare at him, opening Lilah's enclosure and serving her the mouse. "It's my job title. I study insects. I had a job at the lab but then got this idea for a research project. So I quit the lab. It was too many hours, and my focus shifted specifically to Lymantria dispar," I explain my predicament to him. Not like he actually cares.

"*Which is?*" he emphasizes.

"The study of spongy moths. You have just walked into half

my research project." I spread my arms out, gesturing to the map. A smile spreads across my face. I love this stuff.

"And here I thought I just walked into your apartment," he jokes.

I side-eye him. "If you can't handle it, the door is literally right there." I gesture to the door.

He's silent for a moment and glances at the door and then back to me. "Nope, I'm not leaving."

"Want to feed Lilah?" I ask him, feeling cautiously optimistic.

"*No*, but I see now that the overalls and Birkenstocks fit." He eyes me up and down.

He did not just check me out.

"Fit?" My eyebrow angles up.

"*You*," he says, glancing at me again. Oh, I get it.

"Ah, indeed." I chuckle.

"Well, should we get going?" he asks.

"This is your last out. You sure you want to do this?" I ask, collecting my Aztec fanny pack from the kitchen counter.

"Let's do it." Clarke grabs ahold of my hand and leads me out of my apartment.

"So where are we going?" I ask Clarke as we descend the stairs back to his sports car.

"The Bean." He looks at me, smiling, and then looks to our hands and drops his. "There's probably not any paparazzi at your apartment," he says.

"Yep, probably not. Well, let's go. First date day!" I open the door for myself, and when we get inside the car, I tease him, "You know, for the record, I believe the guy should open the car door for the girl." I wink at him, and he nods.

"Noted."

Here we go.

Chapter 10

As we approach the Bean hand in hand, I can admit that while it doesn't feel natural to be holding his hand, it also doesn't feel the worst. The Bean is covered by tourists galore. He tells me to pose in front of it, and so I try and look "trendy." Though, I am thirty-one, and I don't know if I am that anymore. I try and stay up-to-date on the lingo from my sis, but we don't talk all that often. Which leads me to find things out by myself. For instance, the term slay does not mean to fight someone and win. *Whoops.*

I take note from the young women around me and do a pose. He holds his phone out to take a picture of me, and it reminds me. He still doesn't have my number. We'll have to fix that one of these days.

As I'm posing, I'm suddenly distracted by the most beautiful furrow spider. I inch closer to it, trying not to startle it. It's not every day I catch sight of an orb weaver. I don't know what this spider is doing in the concrete jungle, but it would love my garden. I wonder if I can put it in a cup or something temporarily. What do I have?

As if the spider guesses my plan, it starts crawling away from me. I follow it to the other side of the Bean, squeezing between people to follow its trail.

"Wow! You, little lady, are angry. You know my spider Shifty does this too. But I'm not going to hurt you." I stick a dollar bill out to the fat spider on the Bean. Girls around me scream wildly when they realize what I'm doing. They squeal and jump into their men's arms.

Clarke comes out of nowhere, grabs ahold of my wrist, and spins me into him. He kisses me gently, mouth closed. My eyes widen, but then I remember we are in public, and *yes, I am the one in a relationship with Clarke Washington who plays professional basketball.*

He lets me go, and we both lightly smile. He puts his hand at the small of my back, and we turn around, gazing once more on the Bean. I take in the scene around us—lots of women of all ages have their phones out, taking pictures of us. It is a bit uncomfortable. I've never been famous before—in fact, I've been fine flying underneath the radar.

Oh, speaking of underneath! I walk back underneath the Bean to find the spider again.

"Dang it, it ran off. You scared it!" I slug him in the arm and watch him nervously glance around at others.

"Wait, I get it," I whisper harshly.

I get it.

He interlocks our fingers together and pulls me away from the Bean, down closer to the street. "I thought I heard clicking of cameras. Were you trying to cover up my weirdness so the paparazzi couldn't see? Am I too weird for you?"

"Maybe? I mean, the bug thing is kinda weird, Rose Petal."

He rubs at his neck.

Wrong answer.

"Yeah, *Washington*? Well, not to me." I jerk my hand away from his and whistle for a taxi.

The taxi arrives, and he steps in front of me for a moment. Right when I think he's going to try and stop me, he opens my car door for me.

I slide inside. "Thank you," I'm able to mumble to him. He shuts the door, and all I can think is, *That's not exactly what I had in mind.*

***

It's late, and I'm watering the bushes at the garden. I should be heading home, but I love sunsets at the garden, and I could use some cheering up after today. It sucks to be the source of someone's embarrassment. Unfortunately, I know the feeling all too well. That's why I left today. I didn't feel like I had a choice when I was growing up with it all, but now, I won't let people treat me that way. I don't put up with it. It's unacceptable.

Maybe today really was good riddance, and maybe that's for the best. Right as this thought travels across my mind, bright lights pull into the parking lot.

I focus back on the hose. I don't want to talk. I hear his car door shut and footsteps stirring up the gravel.

He stands on the opposite side of the gate and pleads with me, "I'm sorry. I panicked. My life has been image-based for so long, I forgot how to just be a person looking at a spider on the Bean. I'm sorry, Rosie."

I didn't expect myself to talk, but my body wills a response. "I don't think you'll be able to do this. We're too different. You are famous, and even in my own family I am infamous for being weird. You don't want that for your reputation." I shake my head, avoiding eye contact.

"This will probably be good for my reputation—a down-to-earth girl on the outskirts of the city." That sounds like an attempt to make me smile. It didn't work. "Besides, remember, this is how you'll get your research money from the garden taking off, and I'll maybe get into your brother's good graces again," he reminds me of the deal.

I turn off the hose and walk slowly towards the gate.

"No one is going to believe you *like* me," I explain.

"The public is already hooked on the gossip," he encourages me.

"Yeah, but when they come to the garden, I need to be working. I can't have you holding my hand, hugging me, or kissing me while I'm working here. People won't sense any chemistry between us unless we're touching," I explain to him.

"What do you mean?" he asks, hooking his hands into the chain gate.

"Have you never seen one of those cheesy romance movies on tv?" I question him.

He shrugs.

"I'm talking about the glances," I whisper to him.

"The glances?" he asks.

"Yes, occasional glances, longing looks, shoulders brushing, blushing, smiles from across the room—that sort of thing!" I lay my hand across my heart and do a little twirl in place, dreamily looking into the sky.

"If we don't have that, people will suspect something is up," I say, looking back at Clarke.

"Okay, noted." He nods, making intentional eye contact with me.

"No, no, that stuff has to come naturally," I reinforce my point.

"Are you saying you want me to fall for you?" He laughs, mocking me.

"WHAT?" I scoff. "No! I'm saying we need to actually hang out and get to know each other a little more, like you said in the beginning. But like, without the paparazzi, without touching. So we can …" I twiddle my thumbs.

"Become friends?" he asks, trying to steal my eye contact again.

"Maybe? At least until this is over, then we can shake hands, respect each other's journeys, and move along, knowing we both helped the other out. What do you think?" I wonder aloud.

"That sounds like a good idea. Do we need to draw it up in a contract?" he asks, smirking.

"Hey, you said you hadn't watched any of those movies?" I point at him, a grin threatening to appear.

"No, I didn't; you assumed." He crosses his arms across his chest.

"Ugh, okay, but no, we don't need a contract. After all, I have known you for years."

"Does that mean you trust me?" He smirks.

"No." I glance up at him, and my gaze lingers a second too long. I clear my throat and break our eye contact.

"I need to finish the watering." I turn around, since everything is settled.

"I'll change that," he hollers as if accepting a challenge.

"We'll see," I whisper under my breath.

We'll see.

Chapter 11

It's a rather warm day, again. Usually by this time in Illinois, the weather has gotten the point. The cooler nights begin, and the leaves change color. But for some reason, this September, the cooler nights are stunted. It feels like an extended summer, but I'm ready for fall.

I'm preparing the garden for its reopening. The blasted welcome bridge is finally fixed. New paint has been applied to the barn, and roses have been placed upon the trellis arch. The roses are called Carding Mill and Phoenix. They're peach-colored roses with pink undertones. Very different than your typical store roses; usually red is for love, yellow is for friendship, and white is for honor.

I am taking a step in the right direction today as I put my trust in Clarke to accurately paint hearts on the wooden entryway leading into the garden. For a while, I monitored him closely until he insisted I was making him too nervous. I reluctantly agreed as I spotted his hand jittering.

I walked back to the entrance to get to work on the chalkboard in the welcome booth. We've both been working in our respected places for about an hour. I've written the prices per dozen roses and important instructions for picking.

I step back to look at my handwriting and smile. It looks really nice. This place is really coming along. Sweat drips off my forehead from the humidity. I need a break. I reach into the cooler to bring Clarke a water bottle too. I begin my trek over to his side of the garden, and as soon as I turn left, I run right into him.

"*Oof.*"

His arms steady me. "Whoa, what are you doin'?"

I step back, reaching my hand out between us. The waters are ice cold, thanks to my cooler. He grabs the water bottle. "Thanks!" He takes a sip, and as he replaces the cap, he heads to the welcome booth.

"Nice, Rosie. You have neat handwriting," he says, and I beam with pride. *Heck yeah, I do.* "But," he adds.

"What do you mean, but?" I roll my eyes and place my hands on my hips.

"I was just going to say you should add a hashtag too." He points up to the chalkboard and then takes another sip of his water. I want to ask why, but before I get a chance to, he speaks again. "So when people are here, they can take pictures and use the hashtag on social media. It will get it trending," he says.

"You and social media." Sarcasm drips from my lips, though I suppose he's got a point.

He doesn't miss his chance to spar with me. "You and none."

"Hey, I have Instagram," I defend myself.

"Oh, I remember." He smirks.

"But, in my opinion, there is no point. It just distracts you from real life and real connection." I twist my foot in the dirt and cross my arms across my chest.

He chuckles, shaking his head at my comment. He chugs the rest of his water bottle and crushes it. He shoots it into the recycling bin. I try and do the same with mine. I fail miserably. He takes my fail and slam dunks it. *Show-off.*

"So, since we're hanging out right now, tell me, what are some things we have in common?" he asks, leaning against the welcome booth.

"I'm going to inspect your hearts," I say nonchalantly.

"Very well, now answer my question." He gets off the booth and follows close behind me. He seeks an answer and probably a pat on the back for the pretty hearts, but I'll see if he's earned it.

"I think we would have more luck counting the things we don't have in common ...," I answer him, briefly speaking over my shoulder.

I reach up and realize my mistake. I can't possibly reach this archway without a ladder. I hop up to try and blot out a little extra paint dripping down off one heart. But I can't get it.

"Here, let me." His arm shoots up, and I feel like a little bird in his large, manly shadow. I may or may not notice his subtle scent of cedarwood and spice mixed with sweat. I also may or may not have just leaned into him, just a smidgen, for just a moment. But as his arm comes down, it bonks me on the head. *It's fine.*

"Oh, sorry," he apologizes, rubbing my head. This reminds me of when we were kids and shakes me out of my mini moment of infatuation.

"I mean, I hate sports," I spew out to distract myself from him.

His eyebrows furrow. "You always came to our games," he

states, questioning my stance.

I blow out air and tuck a flyaway hair behind my ear. "Psh, shows how much you noticed. I always had my nose in a book."

He sighs. "Fair. But you might like basketball if you gave it a chance." He sticks his hands into his shorts' pockets.

I shoot back, challenging him, "You might like bugs if you gave them a chance."

"Fine, I'll try bugs if you try basketball." *Well, that answer surprises me.*

"Ugh." I roll my eyes once more.

"Ugh back at you," he says, moving closer to me, brushing his elbow against my shoulder. "Are the hearts acceptable to the boss lady?" he asks, smiling at me.

"They are. Just this one needs a little extra help. Let me go get my ladder." But before I can even turn around, he says, "I have a better idea. Here, take this." He hands me the bucket of paint that I gave to him earlier. As I take it, he bends down in front of me, his back to me.

"What?" I question him, an eyebrow extended.

"Rosie, just jump on my back, and I'll give you a boost." This act, so innocent, has my heart pounding against my chest.

"I don't know …" I hesitate.

"Come on, it'll be faster this way, and then we can get out of here. It's hot." He ushers me over.

My eyes betray me as they linger on his strong calf muscles and lean muscular arms. And his athletic back. I take a shuddering breath.

He must hear me as his next question is, "Are you cold?"

"What? No, psh no, you weirdo. Like you said, it's hot out here."

Indeed, it is.

"Rosie, come on. It's me," he says once more as he encourages me to jump on his back. "It's not a piggyback ride, just a boost." He laughs, once again ushering me to get on.

"Alright," I say, holding on tight to the paint can. I climb onto his back and wrap my legs around his waist. I hook one of my arms over his shoulder to keep myself steady. As he lifts me, I feel butterflies in my stomach. It's from the elevation change. Surely that's all it is.

"Okay, here ya go." He holds onto my thighs to keep me steady enough to fix the heart. I dip the paintbrush into the blush paint and fix up the only one in need of correction.

"There," I sigh. He lets go of one of my legs to take the paint can from me. He places it on the ground and then bends down to let me slide off.

As I do, he turns to face me. And gracious, I swear the good Lord has turned up the heat in Naperville, even just in the last hour. Surely. *Surely, that's it.*

I need more water. I feel parched.

"Thank you," I say, desperate for my thirst to be quenched.

"You're welcome; it's the least a tall guy can do." I nod as he smiles.

I skip over to the cooler, taking out a water and chugging it. He walks back to the welcome booth with me.

"Okay, I'll try bugs if you try basketball." His negotiation doesn't get past me.

He stretches out his hand to me, seeking a compromise. I inhale and take in the sight of the rose garden, peering at all the help he selflessly offered today. As I exhale, I stick my hand out to meet his in a shake.

I nod. "Okay, that sounds fair. You've got a deal."

He takes his hand out of mine and smiles at me. "It's

wonderful doing business with you. Oh, and Rosie, I'm not feeding Lilah."

"She's a reptile, not a bug. You clearly did not pay attention in basic biology class sophomore year," I tease him. He scoffs, and as he is about to deliver a comeback, I beat him to it, "Or maybe you've had too many basketballs to the head." I poke the side of his head, since that's all I can reach, and he laughs.

"Touché, Rosie. Touché." He tips his head back and laughs.

Chapter 12

❦

"When you said try basketball, I thought you meant playing basketball, not watching your last practice before preseason starts." I cringe as he tosses a kernel of popcorn into his mouth. All six foot seven of him is sprawled out on my pleather sofa, except he has to bend his knees to fully fit. We talk as I feed my critters. He wants me to come to his practice. Claims it will be good, and most importantly, more convincing if his girlfriend is in attendance. I'm not sure about that. I take ahold of my dishrag and wipe down my countertops.

Sara is coming over tonight. She's been texting me like crazy, trying to get the scoop. She may be in her thirties, but she's actually quite with-it when it comes to trends and social media. Unlike moi. Instead of keeping her in the dark, Clarke and I both decided to invite her in on our scheme. I know that's not how it typically goes in the movies, but realistically, I think this way will work best for us. After all, this is *indeed* real life. Real life, yet we're still scamming people with a fake relationship.

Yeah, that makes sense. 'Kay. Enough of that thought tunnel.

Sara gives me her secret knock, and I don't ask, I just open the door for her. She stomps in; her lavender-colored hair is sopping wet. Mid-September storms have hit Northern Illinois. She throws her soaked crossbody bag into my sink. That's one way to do it. She kicks off her flip flops and twists her wet hair into a claw clip.

"You," she points at Clarke, "and you!" and then at me.

Clarke places his hand on his chest, feigning innocence, and I look at her with a face that says, "who, me?"

"You two are *definitely* not dating." She laughs, looking between us.

"Why are you laughing? We could totally be dating." I wander to my sofa and sit on the arm. He moves his legs over, and I pat my hand against one of his shins. He looks at me and then her, offering an awkward smile.

"Yeah, we could totally be," he agrees with me.

"Nope, not happening. For one, she just patted your shin. Patting is for grandparents only," she rambles, and I pick up my hand from his shin. My face goes cross; I think about it, and she's right. I make a mental note that *pats=grandparents.*

"Besides, he looked at you just now like you burned him. Which means he's not used to your touch," she interrogates us.

"It's not that; it's our burning passion," he says, sitting up on the sofa.

I glance at him with judgment. "Really?" I mouth to him.

"Okay, yeah, we're not," I confirm to Sara.

"But yet, we are." Clarke stands up and walks up close behind me.

"What?" Sara inquires.

We explain the situation, and she blinks at us. Her jaw stays

56

ajar, and finally, she speaks, "You guys have got to be kidding me." She smiles, a spark in her eye.

"I was tired of all the rejections, S. This happened so accidentally, but it's just continued to spiral, so we decided to just let it happen. Not correct anything, and maybe by letting it happen we not only help my grandparents, but also my research project!" I didn't get into the legal advice part because that's not my story to tell. Though, truth be told, I don't even know the story myself.

Sara sighs, "While this is all crazy … it's also pretty exciting. Rosie, even if you just get dating practice from this and no money, that would be great for you."

I'm mortified by her statement. "What? Sara, I'm not desperate for dating practice."

"But maybe you should be …," Sara says.

"Hey!" I toss the throw pillow at her, and Clarke just backs up and lets us go after each other.

"What's in it for you, Mr. Big Name Basketball Player!?" Sara glances back at Clarke.

"Maybe earning some atonement with the St. Clair family," he says, catching me off guard a bit. I furrow my brows and look at him. What is this about? It's the first I've heard of it.

"This could do it." She nods and reaches out for my hand and then Clarke's. She steps between us and pulls our arms closer together. As our knuckles brush together, she places our hands together and backs up.

"You guys have work to do if anyone is going to believe this," she says, staring at us awkwardly holding hands in my living room.

"Told you." I bump my hip into Clarke.

"And how do you suggest we show chemistry?" he asks Sara.

Sara gives me a smile, and I know she is up to no good. I'm nervous to be her test subject.

"Okay, you need to follow some rules. For instance: #1: Create a Backstory, #2: Display Affection and Be Consistent, #3: Have Fun, and #4: Communicate Well. Or else, no one will feel any connection between you two. Oh, and don't forget the glances." She writes up the rules on a sheet of paper.

Clarke leans over and whispers in my ear, "I thought we weren't going to need a contract."

I bump my hip into him once more. "Shh! She's got a point." I nod to Sara and look up at Clarke.

"Oh, come on, people already believe it! Some accidental strategic moves on our part has already sealed the gossip. We're in," he continues to explain, using his hands to reinforce his point.

"You may be in, but you'll want to stay *in*," Sara explains.

"Fine, teach us then." Clarke shrugs and stands beside me; we're still holding hands. All I can think about is how my hand is getting clammy. I need to let go of his hand before this gets any more awkward.

I let go of his hand and wipe mine on my sweatpants. His eyes go to the disconnection and then to me.

"My hand was getting clammy," I whisper, "sorry!"

He facepalms himself, and Sara rolls her eyes. "Come on, Rosie, to the public eye that's going to look like you're repulsed by him."

"But I'm not repulsed by him, and besides, we're not in the public eye. We're in my living room," I defend myself.

"This is going to be harder than I thought." She blows out a breath.

Now it's my turn to roll my eyes.

"Okay, face each other. Chop, chop!" Sara snaps her fingers at us as we turn to each other and follow her instructions.

"Now stare lovingly into each other's eyes," she says. I can tell from my peripheral that she places her hand on her heart.

Clarke and I gaze at one another, but it quickly turns into a staring contest.

"Okay, you guys. You have to blink. You look like freaks," Sara judges us.

Clarke and I hold back laughter as best as we can.

"Closer, closer," Sara says.

"Any closer and his shirt is going to be up my nose!" I exclaim. His chest rumbles beneath me.

"Try it one more time; come on, you guys. Channel a longing glance." We stand toe-to-toe, and I look up at him—this angle is so awkward. Either Sara's ideas are failing or maybe we're just not meant to be.

Sara sighs and turns around for a second. Clarke leans down and whispers in my ear, "Try not to smile, ready, go!" He stands back and winks at me.

Okay, he's on. I may not have played sports, but I love a good challenge.

Sara turns again and begins hovering around us, like we're some sort of prey. We are right under her nose. Our eyes dance around each other's faces, even as we're under her microscope.

"Sara, you're being weird," I say, eyes still locked in on Clarke's.

"I am not being weird! This is how people will know you're in love!" she squeaks out. "By the—"

"Glances," Clarke and I say in unison, "we know, we know."

Clarke gently moves his hand to my waist, and Sara gasps, "Yes! That's what I'm talking about, Clarke!"

My heart flickers for a moment at his touch. But I rein it in so I don't smile. I wonder for a moment why he did that? Was he just appeasing Sara? Before my mind can finish that thought, I burst into laughter. It's so unexpected. Clarke's move was strategic—he set his hand there so he could move up seconds later and tickle me. How does he know I'm most ticklish on the left side of my stomach?

I keel over in laughter, and he declares, "Ah-ha! I win!"

"You two! Neither of you will win if you don't take this seriously. I swear. You're giving me flashbacks from high school with your goofy antics."

I furrow my eyebrows, trying to think of the memory she's referring to.

Summer 2007

My family took a camping trip every year. We'd go to the lake, bring tents, and my grandparents would plan relay races for all us kids. We were each allowed to bring three friends. The number was set at three because Ryder's crew was way too massive. He could choose three and then rotate through them all. That year, he brought Jaxon, Sawyer, and Clarke. I only brought Sara. And Roxy, well Roxy brought Lacy, Amanda, and Nina. Roxy was little at the time, and her and her friends could get annoying. I was fine with keeping to ourselves, but Sara has always been more extroverted than me. She was game with escaping my little sister, but instead of going off on our own, she was intrigued by Ryder and his friends.

One night that trip, we were having a hot dog supper. As my dad and grandpa grilled up the food, Ryder and Sawyer sat on the dock, fishing. That left me, Sara, Clarke, and Jaxon to do the three-legged race. Grandma Irene timed it, and to my dismay, she had us switch partners. When Jaxon and I went through it, we won each time. We were a power duo. But then Grandma wanted me to pair off with

60

Clarke. It was a disaster. He was already so much taller than me, and like I've said, I lack any athletic ability. We fell over and over again in the first few minutes of the race. But he never got frustrated, which surprised me. Ryder has always been super competitive, and I expected the same from his friends. But nope, every time we fell, we fell in different positions, and after the fifth fall, we unanimously decided to just stay down in the grass. We laughed together, and Grandma Irene had to clap to get our attention again.

I smile from the memory and glance at Clarke. I suppose I have forgotten a lot of these memories over the years. I was so introverted in high school—introverted and observant. I loved books and bugs, as I do now. My memories of high school usually include being left out because I didn't play basketball, not being invited to parties because I hated them, not being allowed to get too close to Ryder's friends because he was afraid I had a crush on Clarke, (even though in truth, that was Sara). I sigh. Why do we always *extra* remember the bad stuff? I bet I have more sweet memories like camping that I just need to dig for. My surface-level good memories remind me of all my days at Love in Bloom, the nights in my parents' tree, and some swoon-worthy fictional heroes. But now it's my turn to challenge myself. I want to break the surface and search for more sweet memories.

After all, the reason Clarke's exit hurt so much for my family was because we were all so close. Well, they were. But, if I'm honest with myself, it hurt me too. So I must have collected some sweet memories as well.

As he moves his other hand to tickle my right side, I jump up on my couch.

"It's never the right side, only the left!" I laugh, slapping his hands away.

"Oh, I give up on you two," Sara says as she walks to the kitchen sink to wring out her purse.

"I'll see you *hopeless* romantics later." Sara waves to us and motions to her lips. "Your secret is safe with me."

"Thank you!" we both call after her as she closes the door.

"Man, I don't think we're so bad." I sit on the sofa, and he comes to join me on the other side.

"Well, there's one way to test it." He glances at me, hand reaching into the popcorn bowl again.

I cringe. "Your practice?"

"My practice," he confirms.

I think about it, and I suppose he's right; it'll be good public practice.

"Ugh, okay," I surrender to his idea.

"You and your ughs," he pokes fun at me.

I laugh. "No, no wait! Oh my gosh, remember when those were popular in high school?"

He just shakes his head at me, throwing another popcorn piece into his mouth.

"Okay, I'll go to your practice, and I'll be—"

As I'm about to say *"perfect girlfriend,"* he interrupts me and says, "Yourself."

I glance at him, a smile pulling at my lips. That was sweet.

Instead of my typical sarcasm, I just nod and dig my hand into the popcorn bowl as well.

We sit on different sides of the sofa as we finish the movie, *He's Just Not That into You.*

And I wonder for a moment if people will indeed be able to tell. Or if we'll succeed at our hoax? Only time will tell.

***

I got his number before he left last night, and it's honestly about time. I'm tired of opening Instagram every time I look for a message. I always get distracted and scroll. And I hate scrolling.

Clarke: "**practice is @ 3p. i'll pick u up at 1:30. traffic always be crazy, sorry. oh and btw, no books allowed. ;)**"

I "**love**" his text and head off to dreamland. Until tomorrow.

Chapter 13

There are two things I've never experienced before. And honestly, I can't say my basketball-loving siblings have ever experienced this either. Walking through the, err (tunnel?) in a professional basketball arena. I mean, this is just the practice arena, but still. I don't know what I expected them to practice in, but this is not it. To be fair, my brain was picturing a YMCA gym, and of course they can't practice there. But *goodness!*

Second thing I've never experienced? Walking into a professional basketball practice arena with a bunch of people. Really, super, *very* tall people. We need a song for this montage, like the boys got in high school; that memory plays on repeat as the squeaky sneakers sound against the court.

OPE. This is kind of cool, but you'd never catch me saying that out loud. Especially near my siblings. Over my dead body.

I get seated with the other women who walked in with the guys. I'm assuming this is the wife and girlfriend section. A whistle blows, and the practice begins. I promised him I wouldn't bring a book, and I promised myself that I would act like a doting girlfriend. After one of his teammates makes a basket, his woman in the stands claps and yells, "Yeah, Payson!"

A few other ladies follow suit with their men. "Ace! My man!" And another, "MJ, yes, baby!"

Oh boy. That means I'm next. I could just clap. *I could*. But instead, I ignore the advice of Clarke. He said to be myself, but as he shoots the ball and it swishes through the net, I stand and holler, "Yes! That's my man!"

His head whips around, and his eyes dart to mine in the stands. My heart warms as a small smile breaks through his game face. I give him my biggest smile, with plenty of gumption. I clap my hands together and sit back down. His coach shouts, "Focus, Washington!" I feel bad, yet proud of myself for successfully accomplishing the doting girlfriend.

A few moments later, I try to really pay attention to the game. But it's hard as I'm distracted by whispers.

The whispers are mostly inaudible to me, but I do make out one hushed sentence, "He's dating a granola girl." A group of four ladies glance at me and giggle.

I just smile and pull my overall shorts down a little more over my thighs. If I'm honest, I'm feeling a little self-conscious. After years of rejection and being the weird girl, you'd think I'd be used to it. And I kind of am. But I'm not even sure what a granola girl is. Is it bad? I could search it on the Internet, but I don't want to be on my phone—none of the other women are. Instead of dwelling on it, I try to readjust my focus to the love of the game. Of which I have none.

I can't quite completely get out of my head. In high school, I had Sara, but really that was it. I didn't have a whole lot of girlfriends. They thought bugs were gross, and so then, of course, they thought I was gross. As I glance over at the women who are already looking at me, I cringe inside. I knew this was a bad idea. But right as this thought crosses my mind, one woman walks up to me and says, "Hey, can I sit here? Your name is Rosie, right?" I look up at her, nod, and smile. She's wearing a Chicago shirt, rhinestone earrings, and elaborate fake lashes. She's gorgeous.

"Yeah, sure! And yes! I'm Clarke's girlfriend. Who are you here with?" I ask her.

She points her manicured finger into the practice game. "Ace Maxwell. He's number sixty-two. I'm Mandy!"

"Nice to meet you, Mandy!" I nod toward her and try my best to make small talk.

As we sit and make small talk, we end up laughing together, and before I know it, the clock has run down.

As the guys hit the showers, some loud music starts playing. Mandy tells me she has to go, and most of the girls follow suit to go meet their guys outside of the locker room. I should too, but I'm distracted by this music in the gym. It reminds me of those pep rallies back in high school. And suddenly, I'm struck with an idea. I giggle to myself and create a new playlist on my Spotify.

About ten minutes later, the lights flicker, and I grab my crossbody purse, figuring I need to get out of here and go meet Clarke, just like the other women.

As I round the corner, our eyes meet, and he grins. "There's my woman!" he says, grabbing onto my hand and bringing me closer to his body. My hands land on his chest, and I look up at him, beaming. I'm trying to play the part well.

The ladies who are still here look astonished, and one wearing a ring says, "Boy, you two are too cute."

Chapter 13

Her husband—I think this is MJ—slides his arm across her shoulder and adds, "They're still in the honeymoon phase, Gianna."

Clarke moves to tuck me under his arm and slips his hand around me to rest on my hip. I tilt my head up to look at him, and he bends to press a small kiss to my forehead. "Hey, man, no rushing it! We're not even engaged yet, let alone married," he explains to the guy.

"Yep, not *quite* to the honeymoon phase yet," I add to what Clarke is saying.

"But, new? Yes! Fun? Absolutely! Cute? Yes, she is." He squeezes my side, and I squeal a bit, leaning more into him, sliding my hand down his athletic jacket.

"Come on, babe, let's get out of here." He grabs hold of my hand again, and we walk out of the practice arena hand in hand. Some paparazzi stand on the sidewalk and shoot a few pictures of us.

This is working. They believe it.

I grin from ear to ear. Man, I'm proud of us.

"It's working! Can't wait to see the report right in time for the reopening of Love in Bloom tomorrow," he pulls me closer to whisper in my ear. His warm breath against my ear sends shivers down my spine, and before I know it, I reach up on my tiptoes, grab onto his neck, and press my lips against his cheek.

He glances down at me, and while his look may look endearing to the passing stranger, I know he's probably thinking the same thing as me. Which is, *what was that?* The only problem is, I cannot provide an answer.

***

"So, what did you think?" he asks me as we climb into his Lamborghini.

As I click my seatbelt in, I place my crossbody purse on the floor mat.

I shrug, but a simple smile plays at my lips. "I mean, it was like a basketball game."

"Rosie, it wasn't *like* a basketball game. We were playing basketball."

"I know that. I just mean I've watched many basketball games in my life, and this one wasn't much different," I say but then bite my tongue. I'm lying a little bit. I didn't have quite as big of a desire to read on my Kindle app during that practice. I would assume that has something to do with Clarke, and this … unique friendship we're growing. He intrigues me. Plus, I was focused on the assignment of being a doting girlfriend. And I for one always loved assignments and projects in school. That was probably it.

"Oh, I see." I hear some disappointment in his voice after hearing my observation.

"But hey, after the practice, when you guys hit the locker room? I heard the loud music start playing, and well, I felt nostalgic." I scroll through my phone and throw him a teasing glance. "You ready?" I ask him while hooking my phone up to his Bluetooth.

"Oh no." He chuckles and eyes me.

"Oh *yes*." I slyly smile. "I made a playlist for you. Maybe you can play it during a workout or to pump yourself up in the locker room before a game." I giggle, hovering my finger above the playlist.

"Wow really? Rosie, that's really nice," he starts but then pauses. "Wait, why are you laughing?" He chuckles nervously.

"Don't say thanks until you listen." I press play on the first song.

As the title pops up on the screen, he hollers, "Oh, you didn't!"

"That's right; let's go back to high school pep rallies! Aye!" I say throwing my hands up to the window … and to the other window.

"You don't seem like the kinda girl who listened to this!" He roars with laughter, hitting the steering wheel with his hand.

"Oh, I didn't, but that doesn't mean I didn't hear it at the pep rallies, basketball games, or my brother's outdoor court. Every. Single. Summer." I smirk at him.

"Is this Chris Brown and T-Pain?" he asks, and I rub my hands together.

He eyes me again at the stop sign and cringes. "Oh gosh, what else is on there?"

"Some classic 2000s." I wink at him, feeling giddy. No more trends for a second, just right back to the days where these were the cool hits.

"Shuffle it." He nods, smiling at me.

I press shuffle, and the next song makes me dance like I was once in escadrille. I was never on the team. I'm just feeling the music.

"*Rosie!*" He emphasizes the *e* as I do my little dance in his front seat.

"You did not just put on Destiny's Child," he says. "Oh yeah, you go girl!" He bobs his head to the music.

I click Next as I need to catch my breath. There was a reason I wasn't on the dance team. I cannot dance.

"Noooo," he shouts, bringing his fist to his mouth, holding the steering wheel with his other hand, "Not "Kiss Me Thru the Phone," by Soulja Boy …"

I throw my head back. "Classic 2008, my sophomore year! Senior Night." My smile is so big it's starting to hurt my cheeks

69

a little.

He shakes his head and looks at me for a moment. "You paid attention to more than you let on, didn't you, Little Rose?"

"Little Rose? Gosh, I haven't heard that in forever. Once again, you are not allowed to call me that if I can't call you Washington." I nudge him in the arm with my elbow. My skin brushing against his for that split second makes my heart skip a beat.

"Man, I can't handle any more of these throwbacks tonight. My face hurts," he says, about to turn the dial.

"Okay, okay just one more … This one is for you, Jaxon, Sawyer, Brock, and my brother." He eyes me quickly and then listens for a moment before slapping his steering wheel again. "Rosalie St. Clair! Not "Basketball" by Bow Wow, Jermaine Dupri, Fabolous, and Fundisha." He begins mouthing the lyrics, and I realize he's right. My face hurts. We have to turn off these throwbacks.

I sway my head to either side. I look at him to steal a glance, but he's already looking at me at this red light.

"What's on your mind?" I ask him.

"So was it really so bad?" he wonders aloud. I assume he's talking about the practice.

"Okay," I look at my hands in my lap, appearing serious, but then, I glance up at him and smile, "you had a good alley-oop."

He laughs. "Do you even know what that is?"

"No," I answer him, my eyes watering from my own laughter.

Man, I'm having so much fun with him tonight. This feels so good. Just hanging out with Clarke. He turns down a street right before we get on the highway. "Where are we going?"

Chapter 14

H e pulls his Lambo into this little lot. The sun is setting, but my eyes catch on two basketball hoops on a rickety little street court.

I side-eye him. "Yeah right."

"Come on, I'll teach you how to shoot an alley-oop." He nudges my arm with his elbow, and I roll my eyes sarcastically.

"We don't have any basketballs." I hope that will deter him. I agreed to watch basketball, not play. This might make me hate it again. My lips curl just thinking of the comments from my past. *Why can't you just be like your siblings, Rosie?*

"I always have basketballs." He breaks me from my thoughts as he opens his door and waves me out as well. He takes one out of his trunk and passes it to me. I catch it because I'm not totally helpless. But I don't like it. Not at all.

But Clarke runs to the court in his jeans and white tee and does a few layups. Basketball still makes me cringe. But Clarke? Who knew that the guy I did everything to get away from at that bar is someone I choose to spend time with now. Yes, yes, we have this deal. Of course, but again, this is fun. Between my research projects, working overtime, taking care of my critters, and happy hours with Sara, I haven't had any unscheduled, unpredictable fun in a very long time. It's nice.

I lean against the chain-link fence, arms wrapped around my middle. I look at the city skyline; it's closer than I've ever seen it. He walks with a bit of a swagger, right up to me. Does he always walk like this? Or am I just noticing it now?

"Come here." He holds out his hand to me, and I grab it. He leads me to the free-throw line and tosses me the ball. He claps and then looks at me, anticipating my shot.

I glare at him, feeling stubborn.

"Aren't you even gonna try?" His hands plead with me, but his words have taken me down an old familiar road, reminding me of how much of a disappointment I am to my father. I hear his voice in my head, *Ryder and Roxie both play on a team, so I know you have it in you too! Aren't you even going to try?*

It's like the air has been snuffed out of me, and I find myself shutting down with him. As I turn to talk back to him, my head turns to the left as I hear a popping noise. Before I can comprehend what is happening, suddenly Clarke's body blasts into mine. He covers my mouth as I scream. He picks me up, shielding my body with his own. He runs us back to his car.

"Rosie, get in the car now, and duck your head down. Hurry," he pleads as his fingers fumble with my door handle as he rushes to open my door. He pushes me in as fast as he can and then runs around the back of his car.

My brain recognizes the noise now. Gunshots.

I'm terrified for him. "Clarke!"

"Get your head down," he orders me, jumping into his seat. He gently shoves my head between my knees. He puts the car

72

in drive and squeals his tires before we can even buckle up. I hear the doors lock and his brakes screech as he blows a stop sign. He's just trying to get us out of the neighborhood and onto the highway.

"What the heck, Clarke! What was that?" As we ascend the ramp to the highway, I click my seatbelt into place and bring my head up again.

"I'm sorry. I'm not for sure, but I think it was maybe …" He blinks, mouth ajar; he looks frightened to be sure.

I point to his seatbelt nonchalantly, and he absentmindedly clicks his on as well. I turn around in my seat and look out the back window. I spy the sun setting between the skyscrapers. We were so close to downtown, and usually, especially growing up, I was never allowed downtown alone. Unfortunately, one thing Chicago is known for is the crime. *Oh*, a realization hits me as the playlist plays "No Air" by Jordin Sparks quietly in the background.

"*Gangs?*" I whisper, answering his half-completed thought.

He nods, calming down a bit as the city gets farther and farther away in his rearview mirror.

"I'm sorry; I shouldn't have stopped in the city. I should have driven out to the suburbs before I stopped. I don't know what I was thinking." His stress has taken quite a toll on his body. His neck is so tense, I can see one vein in particular; it's almost throbbing.

"It's okay, we were having fun," I whisper to him, gently placing my hand on his shoulder.

"No, that was unforgivable. I'm sorry." He shakes his head, holding himself in a prison of guilt.

It's finally a seasonably chilly night in Chicago, and Clarke needs to calm down.

"I have an idea. After you take the Naperville exit, head to the rose garden." I point out the window for him to turn.

"But tomorrow is reopening day! I can just drop you off; that way, you can get plenty of rest." He takes his eyes from the road for one second to look at me.

"Please, Clarke, take us to Love in Bloom. Do you trust me?" I uncharacteristically take hold of his hand that rests against his thigh. I pull it to the middle console and squeeze it. He glances at our hands and then at me.

He gulps and agrees, "Okay."

Chapter 15

"So what are we doing here?" Clarke asks as he puts the car in park.

"Let's take a walk. Come on." I open my door and step out into the breezy evening. He steps out around the car and follows behind me to the entrance.

I sidestep around it, and he calls out to me, "What? Where are you going?"

"Just follow me," I yell over my shoulder at him. The streetlamps of the parking lot are on, and a few security lights at Love in Bloom. But mostly, it's dark. Good thing I know where I'm going. But he is a professional athlete, so I tell him, "But maybe turn on your phone light so you don't step in any awkward holes."

"Got it," I hear him say behind me as the glow of a phone light shows in the grass.

"Where are you taking us?" he asks me.

"You are so nosey." I turn to face him, walking backwards up the hill. "We're almost there; you said you trust me." I nod, eyeing him.

"Okay, okay," he sighs, yet continues up the hill.

As we get to the tippy top, I hear a pleasant sound escape his lips. "Wow."

"Yeah," I whisper, looking onto my grandparents' old property. Sure, it's overgrown with long grass, as it's been a couple weeks, and the house is for sale. But the view.

Fireflies.

Everywhere.

"Let's go." I dip my leg between the barbed-wire fence to slip underneath it.

"Is this illegal? This land is for sale. Maybe we shouldn't trespass?" He hesitates.

"You won't get in trouble if you're with me. This is my family's land. It's for sale, but still theirs," I explain over the fence separating us.

He stands there, just blinking, jaw dropped.

"Well, are you coming or not?" I'm ready to keep walking.

"Okay, yeah," he says. He lifts his leg over the barbed wire and gets to my side unscathed.

"I didn't know tonight would be both basketball and bugs," he says as we walk rather quietly through the field.

"I don't love surprises, but sometimes they make life better." I turn back to smile at him.

"So what are we doing here?" he asks me. I grab the hair tie off my wrist and pull up my platinum blonde waves.

"We're playing a game," I say, winking at him.

"Oh, two games too?" He chuckles, his stare lingering on me for an extra moment.

"Yes, except this one really tests your hand-eye coordination, in the dark." I grin at him in the moonlight. "You better watch yourself, Clarke, I grew up doing this. So even though you're an athlete, you might not win." I run in place, pumping myself up.

"Awfully competitive sounding for someone who didn't play sports," he jeers. "And what exactly are we doing?" he asks as I get into a racing stance.

I shout, "Go!" and take off into the field.

"Go what? Go where? What am I doing?" he shouts back at me. His voice is laced in laughter, and I know it's working. I'm trying to lighten his mood after tonight.

"Isn't it obvious, Clarke? Catch a firefly!" I shout back at him, but once I reach the tall grass, I crouch down, waiting for my prey. Of course I'm not going to hurt the gorgeous things, just catch and release.

I hear footsteps just beyond me, and I know it's game on.

I giggle as I watch him through my spot in the tall grass; he keeps cupping his hands together in the air but missing. I'm not doing much better though, so I really can't give him such a hard time. Truthfully, I haven't done this in years. I did all the time growing up, but it's been a while. Life goes on as an adult.

My grandparents are selling their whole property, other than Love in Bloom, per our agreement. The property is about six acres, excluding the garden. They have a pond, a large oak tree similar to my parents', and a few more grassy hills.

Right as it's quiet, a firefly bobs in front of me. As I go to trap it, I hear Clarke yell out, "Whoa!" I startle and stand instantly to go check on him.

"Clarke? Where are you? Are you okay?" I mean, we are just hanging out by the light of the moon, and there is some uneven ground.

"Rosie, look out!" he yells, and before I know it, I step in the same hole he did, and I'm rolling down the same grassy hill.

"Are you okay?" He army crawls over to me. My blonde hair spills out of my ponytail, and I spit out some grass. I look at him, serious for a moment.

But then two seconds later, my face breaks into a smile, and we are both laughing.

"Who won?" he asks, rolling onto his back, staring up at the clear night sky.

"I'm pretty sure neither of us. Especially since, well, I don't know about you, but thirty has been kind of rough on my body. I'm going to be sore tomorrow." I mirror him, turning onto my back in the grass. We both stare up at the sky.

We stay this way for a long while.

I wrestle between making a joke and trying to dive a little deeper into what happened earlier tonight in the city.

After a few more moments, in fear that I will fall asleep unless one of us says something soon, I choose the safe course.

"Hey, by the way, what's a granola girl?" I wonder aloud.

"You don't know?" He chuckles.

"Um. No. That's why I'm asking you." I lean my shoulder over, and it brushes against his.

"Well, it's a girl who likes the outdoors, books, nature, probably bugs, maybe is a little …," he starts describing.

"Ah, weird?" I swallow hard. I was right—those ladies were judging me.

"No, I was going to say a little like you," he begins, his voice gentle. "Where did you hear the term? Instagram?" he asks, turning his head to look at me.

"The women sitting around me—the girlfriends and wives of other players—they were whispering and giggling," I say as lighthearted as possible, but my eyes betray me as they slightly water. I tilt my head away so he can't see. It's foolish of me to still be so affected.

"Oh, Rosie, I'm sorry." He reaches out to me, his hand landing over mine in the grass.

"Don't be, I'm totally fine. I was just curious about what it meant," I lie through my teeth.

"You really don't care about what people think of you, do you?" he asks half-heartedly. I'm not sure he believes me, but he's at least pretending he does. I appreciate that. Sounds like he's chosen the safe route too.

And as if I'm a confident and successful thirty-one-year-old with all my stuff together, I answer, "What people think doesn't matter."

After one more moment of silence, he sits up. He leans his arms on his knees, hugging them to his chest.

"Thank you," he says out into the open space, but I know he's talking to me.

I keep it lighthearted. "Well, basketball and bugs part one wasn't a total crisis. I'll look forward to the next one." I slip my hand out to him for him to shake.

Shake? What am I thinking?

He glances at my hand, smiles, and nods.

"Right. Let's get you home, Little Rose." He stands and offers me his hands. I take them and give him a sassy look.

"Okay, *Washington*."

Chapter 16

Ring, ring … my phone sounds. I'm video calling Sara at seven in the morning. She reacts how I expect, clicking on her video but then showing me a close up of her lips. "I'll call you later, crazy. It's seven on a Saturday. You've lost your mind." She hangs up the call. I stare into the mirror, unsettled. What am I supposed to do about this? There is only one person who will understand. So I ring him instead.

To my surprise, he answers. He rolls over in his bed, *shirtless*. I try not to notice, but who am I kidding? I do. My eyes travel to his broad chiseled shoulders as white sheets wrap around his chocolatey chest. His head rests on his pillow. He rubs his eyes, blinking and yawning. "What's up, Rosie?"

"Clarke, are you still in bed? The reopening starts at nine thirty!" I nervously begin to chatter.

"I'm getting up now, but what's going on? What is on—" He widens his eyes. I know what he's going to ask, and it confirms my problem. People *will* stare.

"Bug bites. A plethora of them! From the grass last night. I'm such a dummy. I know better. I guess the chilly night just made me forget. But it had been so unseasonably hot this September, so the bugs didn't die. Usually, I use bug spray when I go out there, but last night, I guess I was caught up in the moment with you." I bite my tongue. *Wait …* He clears his throat, and if I'm not mistaken, I catch a smile.

"Are you enjoying this?" I question him.

"Oh no, not at all, cause I'm equally bit up. Just not on my face." He looks down at his chest and moves the sheet so I can see the bites all across his midsection. I cringe. *Eesh.*

"Oh gosh, Clarke! I'm so sorry." I slap my forehead and then sneak a scratch.

"No scratching! Here, I'll come over and help you feed the critters, so you have time to rub anti-itch lotion all over those." He points to my face.

"They're not only on my face either." I'm a little upset, just because I'm worried about how reopening day will go when I look so ridiculous. It looks like I have chicken pox. The crowd will run away from me.

"So many newscasters will be there today." My eyes expand just thinking about it.

"Don't say another word. I'm getting up now and heading to your apartment. Don't freak out. I'll be there soon." He hangs up the call, and I take a deep breath, gripping my sink. It's going to be a long day.

***

Four knocks on my door, and I'm opening it to a very tall man, carrying a box of Krispy Kreme donuts and two coffees.

Yes!

"Oh, Clarke, you're the best!" I say as I gather the food from his hands.

"Come here, you gluten goodness," I whisper to a glazed donut as I open the box and take a whiff.

No, no I have to focus.

"Okay, we only have about forty minutes until we need to leave for the garden, and I have a lot more lotion to do." He looks me up and down. Yes, I look like a crazy person probably, definitely not professional in my PepperAnne pajama shorts and baby blue tank top. Not to mention all the blotches of pink lotion all over my face.

"Okay, you go back to the bathroom and finish doing your hair and makeup." He points me back to my bathroom.

"Not before I save this guy." I scoop up a donut and sink my teeth into it. *Mmm.*

"Save him?" Clarke asks. He's already dressed for the day, and he looks handsome. He's wearing nice jeans, a pastel coral cotton tee, and a gold watch. Tied together with a white ball cap.

"From the big basketball player who might eat him and all his friends," I tease him and walk back to my bathroom.

"What are you going to wear today?" he asks me—his voice carries down the hall.

"I think this V-neck, navy tank top and white shorts," I shout back.

"Okay, the only thing I got out of that is tank top and shorts," he says.

"Oh, come on, Mr. Stylish didn't understand V-neck?" I call over my shoulder as I hear his footsteps approaching the bathroom. He leans his arm up on the door frame and gently leans into it.

We make eye contact in the bathroom mirror as I hold the straightener over the top portion of my hair.

"You think I'm stylish?" he asks me and sneaks in a cheeky grin.

"Oh, come on." I roll my eyes and nod my head toward his reflection.

"Of course you are," I state the obvious.

He smiles as I run the straightener through my thin hair.

"Okay, move. I'm going to shut the door to get dressed now. Were you serious about feeding the critters?" I ask him, doubting he was.

"Sure, point me in the direction of the rat. How many seconds in the microwave?" I gape at him. "What? Mr. Stylish is capable of handling a frozen rodent." He gulps down his coffee and turns back down the hall.

I watch him walk away, a small sizzling sensation in my heart, maybe stomach? *Moths*? Or no, I believe the phrase is indeed *butterflies*.

He hasn't once called, or even hinted at the fact that he thinks I'm weird. And I would definitely put me in that category today. I mean, have you seen my face?

I hear him making a ruckus in the kitchen as I shut the door and pull my outfit off the hanger. I slip it on and finish my hair.

As I'm nearing the last strand, I hear a faint knock on the bathroom door. "You can open it," I say.

He lightly pushes on it, and it glides open.

"Wow," he says.

My heart betrays me again; he's not talking about my clothes. He's talking about all the blotches of pink lotion. Surely. They're everywhere. What am I going to do?

I cringe, reaching my finger behind my shoulder to one of the many spots on my back. "I need to still put lotion back here," I insist; I can barely reach the spot.

"May I?" he asks permission from my reflection in the mirror.

"Oh, what the heck; sure, here." I give him the lotion and cotton ball and lean into the mirror to blend in my makeup. I go ahead and just put foundation over the spots, hoping to hide them altogether.

The cool anti-itch lotion on my itchy skin feels amazing.

"Ahh," I sigh in relief as he dabs on lotion to the bites on my shoulders.

I lift up the hem of my shirt, just to tuck it into my bralette. *Dang chiggers.* Usually, they go for tight spaces and crevices, though clearly this time they didn't discriminate. While I have bites on my face and shoulders, they are especially bad along my spine, at my waist, and my hips.

"Is this okay? I have a few more on my back that are hard to get." My fingers jump to my tucked shirt; if he says no, I'll yank it free. Everything feels so natural with Clarke, I kind of forgot he might be uncomfortable, and that's not what I want. His eyes lock with mine in the mirror, and I catch his Adam's apple bobbing.

"Uh, yeah, yeah sure." He slowly moves his eyes down my back and continues to dab sweet relief onto the bites down my spine.

"The newscasters are going to be there today," I state again.

"Yeah, and how are you feeling about that?" he asks me, focusing on the task at hand.

"Nervous. This isn't really my thing. You know? The cameras, they make me a little nervous," I mumble.

"I'll be right beside you, but also, you should be proud of all your hard work. The garden looks so great. You've really got it back in working order," he says. I feel a stray hair sticking to the back of my arm, and as I reach for it, he finds it first, gently removing it. His fingers brush against the back of my arm, and I shiver. He surprises me by tracing a finger along my jaw. My heart or stomach or whatever it is, is scorching and fluttering like crazy.

His touch nearly takes my breath away. My eyes are pulled to his like a magnet. We stand there, our reflections still as a statue for a moment. My eyes blink, wondering when my body will once more allow me a breath.

"What is happening?" I breathe out, voice barely above a whisper; it takes everything in me to not close my eyes and just lean in …

Whoa. Whoa. Whoa.

"I just saw this one here, under your chin; don't want you to forget it." He rubs a little bite with lotion, and I feel mortified. Here I am, getting flustered, and he's just trying to help me out. Red floods my cheeks, and as he's done dabbing on the lotion, he tosses the cotton ball onto the sink. Though he takes me by surprise, and his finger returns to the spot and begins to tickle me. "Ticklish here?" he asks.

I squirm away from him, squealing, swatting at his chest. That's my answer for him.

"Thanks, Clarke, for all this." I glance up, momentarily caught by him in the doorway.

"Of course." He nods, smiling.

"So we really have to sell it today," he says and backs up from the doorway, giving me space to get around him.

I reach into my coat closet in the front of my apartment. "I think I'm going to wear these Converse. I mean, I'm already wearing a cute outfit, but I also want it to look and feel casual. Kind of like what your outfit says. You've got on jeans and a clean shirt but also a casual backwards hat," I reply to him giddily while digging in my front closet.

"My hat isn't on backwards," he says from behind me.

"Yeah, but it should be. Guys look best with backwards hats," I tease him as I grab my shoes.

When I step out of my closet, I realize my mistake. I'm a great big idiot.

"Like this?" He adjusts the hat so it's backwards, and heat pools in my stomach.

"Um, yep." I have to act like it's not distracting me, not turning my attention to him. Not destroying my insides. *I'm an idiot.*

"Looks good." I swallow and move around him to finish feeding my critters.

"Yep, you too." He clears his throat, rubbing at his neck. "We gotta sell it today, Rosie," he says again. "It will really help you and seal your fate for next season as well."

"Yeah, I know you're right. I think we can do this. I mean, just look at us at the basketball practice and walking to your car. We got this. We got this," I explain to him, while also trying to convince myself to stay calm in this little game we have going on.

Speaking of this game, I'm losing. What did Ryder always tell me in high school? "No falling for my friends." Does that rule still apply even though they have beef? Because if it does, dang it I'm in trouble. This might be even worse, falling for your brother's ex-best friend. Or worse still, falling for your fake boyfriend. Oof.

"Don't worry, Rosie, just some hand holding should do the trick." He winks at me in that stupid, yet delicious backwards hat, and I'm weak in the knees.

"We're good. We're good." I nod, desperately trying to

convince myself.

"Yep, and now we're almost late, so let's go," he says, pointing to my clock. He ushers me out the door.

Okay, okay, it's showtime.

Chapter 17

"Good morning. Wow, Ms. St. Clair, what an exciting reopening day! Tell me about Love in Bloom Rose Farm." There are a few reporters from all different stations out in the parking lot, but this particular one wandered inside the garden. She found me near the welcome booth, and thankfully, I can leave my loyal employee, Renee, in charge of the rose purchases as I walk away to interview. My hands are clammy, and it's not just the Chicago humidity. I am so uncomfortable in interviews, but I decide to fake it till I make it. After all, today I'm dressed out of my usual garb. I look like a professional. Or maybe just a normal thirty-one-year-old? I don't know.

"Well, first, may I just remind the public, this is a place to fall in love. My grandparents, Bill and Irene St. Clair, poured their hearts into the running of this garden. Their marriage is the strongest I have ever known. Back in the day, the public was obsessed with their wholesome union." I give my remarks to the reporter, a huge smile plastered on my face.

"Oh yes, there is a rumor that if you get engaged at Love in Bloom that you will stay married for life," she says giddily.

"Not only that, Katy, but you may just have a brush with fate at our very garden," I reply to her, turning to the camera. I'm directing that comment straight to the audience. Our long-standing marketing ploy. Come here, and you'll find true love, or at least some luck in the love department.

"Oh yes, look at you. Once upon a time a solo Rosie St. Clair, now dating famous basketball player Clarke Washington."

Oh, I should have known she would take it in this direction. But now I'm embarrassed; my grip on faking it till I make it is dwindling.

"How did you score this catch?" she continues. I wince slightly; somehow just the talk of his popularity reminds me of my lack.

"I think I will take this question, as I'm the one with the catch." Clarke swoops in from out of nowhere, right when I need him. I hope the camera didn't catch my wince. He wraps his hand through mine and squeezes. Aw, that was nice of him; he must have seen me struggling. I squeeze his hand right back as a thank you.

He keeps the conversation going as I just look upon him as the doting girlfriend makes another appearance.

"We've known each other since high school, but we only recently reconnected. Actually, since she became the owner of Love in Bloom. So who is to say it's just a rumor?" He holds my clammy hand, and I feel bad for him. My hand feels disgusting.

"Hear that, folks? If your love life is a mess, come on down to Love in Bloom and pick yourself some roses! Maybe things will look up for you. Just look at these two lovebirds." At her words, Clarke turns and kisses my cheek. I grin, pleased that the interview is over.

"Cut. Thanks, you guys; best of luck in your business." The reporter shakes my hand—that poor, clammy hand.

"Thank you for doing a piece on the garden," I express my gratitude.

"Sure, it was his idea. Thanks for reaching out, Mr. Washington. See you on the court this season." She reaches up and places her hand on his shoulder, giving it a squeeze. All this squeezing. Of hands, shoulders, and now I feel as though Katy has just death gripped my heart as she makes me realize I am playing a dangerous game. On the outside, we're faking it—this relationship—for publicity and for Ryder. But on the inside, my heart. Either it's a side effect of being starved of affection for way too many years, or I'm falling for Clarke. I need to get my head on straight, but how can I at the moment, when I spy this reporter flirting with my fake boyfriend?

"Thanks, Katy." Clarke waves to her as she walks off, and that's my cue.

"So, Katy? Is she a close friend of yours?" I ask, trying to be nonchalant.

His smile perks up. "Are you jealous?"

"What? Psh, no, I was simply wondering about your real life." *Busted.* Maybe I am? But if I am jealous, I'm legit equally curious.

"She's not a close friend of mine. She's a reporter who usually covers all things basketball," he explains, running the back of his hand down my arm. His touch sends sparks through me, making it difficult to focus on what he's saying. Does he feel the same electricity between us? Or am I really just starved of affection like I previously mentioned?

"So she just so happened to make roses her priority today?

90

Instead of basketball?" I playfully ask, knowing full well I also owe him a thank you. That news report will surely get even more people out here.

"Well, I mean, I'm here." He smiles, and I nudge him in the ribs.

My phone dings, and I pull it out of my pocket.

Sara: Oh girl, you've got it bad. How are you going to explain this to them? Have you talked to Ryder yet? Your mom and dad always watch Good Morning Chicago, and girl, you guys are front and center this morning.

Picture Attached: Clarke and I, hand in hand, deep in the interview. The image she took, paused right as we glanced at each other.

I feel busted, embarrassed, like I have a crush on the popular schoolboy, and I'm the loser.

Do these feelings ever go away? Like come on, I'm thirty-one, for goodness' sake. We're adults; he can date or fake date whomever he wants. Of course this is just a show for him. *Remember, Rosie,* I tell myself, *he has something to gain from this too. Ryder.*

***

"Longest day ever," I mumble as I push the gates closed behind me.

"You look dehydrated," Clarke tells me. He tosses me a water bottle, but I don't catch it. I'm exhausted, sweaty, itchy, and sore. I should have worn my Birkenstocks.

He reaches down to pick up the water bottle.

"I need another round," I say. He winds up his arm to throw it underhand again, but I put out my arms to stop him. "No! Not of water, of lotion." He swoops in, tucking me under his arm, and walks me to the car. Good thing we rode together this morning because I have zero gumption to drive. I could pass out in this parking lot.

***

"Wha …?" I startle awake to a pecking noise. It's my downstairs neighbor, Mrs. Kraft, with her little dog, Jinky. She's poking her finger into the window. Where am I?

"Are you okay, dear? You should really go inside; it's getting late." She points up my apartment stairs. I'm in the car. I fell asleep in the car, and as I look over, I realize, dude, Clarke left me in here. Pssh, he should have woken me up. I sit up and try and gather myself. My straightened hair is now a frizz bucket poking in all sorts of directions, including some strands stuck to the drool on my cheek. So lovely. I click open the passenger door and thank my neighbor, then I walk up the stairs dragging my feet. I feel so icky.

As I reach for my keys, I realize my door is already open. I cautiously look into my apartment and hesitate. But then I hear his voice, "Rosie?"

"Clarke?" I step in and shut the door behind me.

"Why didn't you wake me up?" I kick off my shoes in the front room and walk across the comfy carpet with my bare feet. I follow the sound of running water down the hallway.

I stop in the bathroom doorframe, and my heart drops along with my jaw.

Am I imagining this? No one can see us. This isn't for the public eye. This is just Clarke, being so thoughtful and so kind.

My eyes tear up a bit; no one has ever done anything like this for me.

"Clarke," is all I can make out. The bathroom light is turned off, there are candles lit along the sink, and I look into my bathtub. The steam bounces off the water, and it's bubbly.

92

"I was going to come back and get you when this was ready." He stands and naturally places his hands on my shoulders. "I figured you could use a relaxing oatmeal bath after our long day. I learned the recipe from my mom when I had poison oak as a kid. I figured it might also work for chiggers." His thumbs rub circles into my muscles, and I wonder if he can tell what he's doing to me. My eyes water, partly because I'm so grateful for this and partly because for me, there's no going back, and I'm terrified he doesn't feel it too. I'm still terrified of rejection.

"I'll let myself out, 'kay? I'll lock it." He squeezes my shoulders again, and his close proximity nearly steals my breath away completely.

As he lets go of me and steps into the hallway, I take one step toward him. His back is towards me. I reach out my hand, narrowly missing his shirt, and then I yank my hand back in before I ruin this.

I can't. I like this too much. *Us.* I can't ruin it by some silly crush.

"Thank you, Clarke," I say, leaning against the doorjam. I wave my hand at him as he puts on his shoes to leave.

"Goodnight, Rosie." He nods to me, and I hear the door click.

I look over my shoulder at the bath and cannot wait to dip my feet into it and relax. But how can I possibly relax? I most definitely have caught feelings for my brother's ex-best friend.

I pull out my phone to text Sara:

Rosie: Yeah, I'm in trouble.

Chapter 18

I wake the next morning to several texts:

Sara: **Uh, duh.**

Clarke: **good morning, wanna catch dinner tonight?**

Mom: Young lady, I think we need to have a talk. Can you come over for dinner?

Hmm, who do I want to have dinner with? Clarke or my parents? Hard choice between getting a lecture or hanging out with my crush and possibly, yet probably, falling even harder. One option is definitely more dangerous. *Hmm.*

I text them back in order of received:

Rosie: I'll text you later, S.

Rosie: Let's do it. Downtown Naperville?

Rosie: Sorry Mom, I have plans tonight. Maybe next weekend?

As I'm about to close my phone, I get two more texts:

Clarke: sounds great, txt me later on where to meet you.

Roxy: ry is gonna be furious...

I smile as I read Clarke's, holding my phone to my chest, then I hold it back again to read the rest of my sister's text.

Roxy: ry is going to be furious when he finds out. what are you doing, sis? you've never been one to play with fire. you're all over social media.

My face scowls. Did mom put her up to this? She never, ever, *ever* texts me. But I suppose if I'm disappointing the family, *again*, they'll pull out all the stops.

It's a shame people can't just be happy for me. I always have to be doing something wrong. I think about the degrees I've pursued, the research project, basketball … I pull my hair into a ponytail and put on a crew neck sweatshirt with my overalls. Today, I'm wearing Birkenstocks.

I put on some mascara, and as I look into the mirror, I realize this is the first time I see myself as normal and not weird. I'm an adult with an interest in bugs and Birkenstocks, and that's not weird. It's who I am. I'm starting to realize my personality isn't a burden. I just have to find the right people because they'll love the real me. Like Sara. I know my family loves me; I just break down every single one of their expectations. But maybe I need to stop focusing on their expectations and just thrive on my own.

I smile as I walk to the pantry to scoop up the dry dog food for my Bobbles. I spy the time on the microwave: 9:15 a.m. I have to get to the garden.

***

"Man, I'm exhausted," I say as I spot Clarke's car in the parking lot.

"The day after reopening day I'm sure just felt like another reopening day." He closes his door and comes over to meet me.

"It was a success for sure, less televised though, which was nice." I offer him an easy smile and naturally let my hands slip around his waist.

"What?" he says. His hands hold onto my elbows as he looks down at me.

"Thank you for your help." I'm momentarily blinded by the bright parking lot lamp and can't see his face. It makes me nervous. Does he not like my arms here? Is it too much?

"Sure." He releases my elbows, and I decide to break my arms free from his waist. He surprises me by catching one of my hands. He slips his fingers through mine. "Can I buy you dinner?" He glances at me, pulling me to his side. Relief floods me. Even if this is just part of our game, I'll bask in it for now.

"Sure, just nothing fancy, cause I'm a hot mess from today." I watch his chest rumble, and I realize he's laughing at me.

"What? You saw me yesterday. It was just as humid today. Cooler, but humid," I plead my case as we get into his car and head down to Naperville's main street strip.

He helps me out of his car, and I say, "For sake of appearances, I should probably continue to hold your hand." Why did I say that? *Seriously?*

He grins. "Yeah, okay." He walks with a type of basketball swagger I've seen before. He's so confident, and then there's little old me.

Hand in his, walking with him down the street. I pull on his hand to stop him as we approach a little cafe.

"Okay, have you had Boba tea?" I ask, feeling giddy.

"I thought we were getting dinner?" he asks me, turning to look at me and at the cafe, which has a neon orange Open sign in the window.

"We will but answer the question." I bounce on my heels.

"No, I haven't," he answers.

96

"Alright, come here." I yank on his hand once more and lead him into Bubbly Teas Cafe.

"Do you trust me?" I ask him as he looks at the menu in wonder. He glances at me. "Yeah." He nods, a big smile on his face. I grin at his *yeah*.

"We will have two brown sugar lattes with tapioca pearls." He tries to speak, and I just raise my finger, simultaneously throwing a twenty-dollar bill on the counter.

"Thank you." He nudges my shoulder.

I hear a few younger girls giggling, but I don't turn. He does and pulls me a little closer into him. I'm not sure what he saw, but I go along with his lead. Once we get our drinks, Clarke pulls me with him to a corner booth and lets me scoot in first, then he sits right next to me.

"Clarke," I furrow my brow, "did you forget? I'm all sticky and gross from the humidity today … Why don't you sit across from me instead?" I explain to him as our shoulders brush. I'm sure I smell gross.

"Phones," he whispers to me.

"People are taking pictures of me?" I gulp.

"Us," he corrects me.

"Well, we are in our hometown now, so I guess that makes sense." I take a sip of the drink.

"This wasn't my hometown," he says. I don't miss his tone of voice, and I wonder what he's not telling me.

I decide to keep it lighthearted for now, with all these cameras around.

"Well, it basically was—you were at my house all the time." I smile, and he does too, but his doesn't reach his eyes.

He takes his sip of the boba and coughs. "It's like drinking caviar, but it tastes sweet."

"Lots of people say that." I laugh, leaning into him.

"You ready to get out of here?" he asks me, our faces mere inches apart.

His hand sits on my knee under the table, and he gives it a little squeeze.

All the squeezing.

Gee whiz.

His touch catches my breath, but I smile and nod. "Yeah, let's go."

***

We had some pizza at a casual place across the street for dinner. It was delicious. I noticed they even have gluten free pizza there, so I'll have to take Sara there sometime. He asked me if I wanted to go for a cruise around town, but I suggested we take my car to keep a low profile. A red Lambo driving around with his basketball number on the back windshield? Yeah, I wonder who that belongs to?

"So, what kind of music does this granola girl listen to?" he asks me, and I face him for a moment at the red light.

"This is one of my favorites right now." I push play on my Spotify playlist. "Hozier's "Work Song." I like Hozier, Bon Iver, The Lumineers, but also, I like Maddie & Tae, Morgan Wallen, and Zach Bryan." I shrug.

"Those are all pretty different," he chuckles.

"Eh, well maybe I'm not a granola girl then; maybe I'm just Rosie St. Clair," I say, driving along the side street, turning into my grandparents' property.

"You want to do this again?" he asks me, eyes wide, looking at my bit-up face no doubt.

"I'm smarter this round." I pull out some bug spray from my console.

"You were thinking ahead? Planned this? Hmm? Almost like we're on a date." He looks at his lap and then up at me. I can't breathe.

"I … I …" I can't *breathe.*

"Rosie, relax. I'm just giving you a hard time. I'm glad you have bug spray. Girl, you are trippin'. Come on, get out." He ushers me out of the car, and I take a deep breath.

I'm losing it. I'm losing my cool. I'm too old for these feelings. I feel like I'm in high school again. I see the large oak on the side of their property, and it gives me an idea.

I spray my body with the bug spray and then throw the can at Clarke. I take off running.

I hear the aerosol can spray as I use my legs to carry me to that tree.

"Hey, unfair advantage!" he calls out after me.

"Keep up!" I call back to him.

As I reach the tall grass, I say a silent prayer that I don't get any more chiggers. I take long strides to the large oak tree.

I stand at the bottom of it and let the breeze lift my ponytail off my back. I breathe in the night air, closing my eyes for a moment.

I startle as I feel his arm graze over mine. My heart beats erratically, but I keep my eyes shut, taking deep breaths.

He surprises me with his next line, his voice is low. "Do you remember graduation night? You were sitting out in your parents' tree, reading a book."

My mouth gapes open. When I replay that night in my mind, I could have sworn Washington thought he was alone. I decide to keep this going. "Yeah, you came out and told me goodbye. I … I thought you were crazy. Drank too much at the party or something," I explain.

"No, I don't drink, never did," he says, digging his shoe into the dusty ground.

"And then the next day, you were gone. Like gone, gone. And nobody knew what happened until the guys heard about it on ESPN. You got called up to the big leagues," I say to him.

We're both just looking forward, not at each other. That would be too much. "That's what they say in baseball." He chuckles.

"It's the same thing," I say.

"If you say so. It was just Duke," he answers me.

"Oh, come on. I don't even watch basketball, and I know there is no such thing as *just* Duke."

"I got my ticket," he says, his voice absent of emotion.

"You should have told them goodbye, Clarke." He shifts his arm so it's no longer touching mine, and I get brave. For I scoot closer to him, so we touch arms once more.

"I didn't want them to think I thought I was better or rock the boat," he says, looking ahead at the tree. I open my eyes and look up at his.

"Yeah, but you shouldn't have just left. He never forgave you." I hold his forearm, and he works his jaw before speaking again.

"He never forgave me cause I stole his dream."

"Think that if you want, but I think it's cause you left and ghosted him. You were like a brother to him," I explain.

"You don't think I think about that? Your family was everything to me!" His angry tone surprises me, and I let go of his arm, bringing my hand back to my side.

A few moments of silence pass.

I'm not sure where to go from here, but I can see his eyes, glassy in the moonlight.

I try to lighten the mood, bring him back.

"Even the annoying little sister?" I ask, turning to him, a smirk crossing my face.

"Roxanne *was* pretty annoying." He chuckles, remembering.

I scoff, "I meant me."

"Oh, ha."

"See, I was invisible." I smile, but now I'm the one trying to hide the pain in my eyes.

"You weren't invisible." He turns to me.

"I *was*." I smile again and take a few more steps towards the tree in the tall grass.

"Rosie …" He reaches for me, and I turn, my blonde flyaway hairs blowing in the chilly wind. My back is to the large oak. I search his face; my eyes are glistening. I can't help it; the moon is reflecting in my dark brown eyes.

"You didn't only bring books to our basketball games. You brought *Best Insect of the Month* magazines and a magnifying glass. When the guys were at your house, playing video games late into the night, you'd climb out your window and climb down the fence, thinking no one noticed you. You'd run out to the tree with your … *what* I'm not sure, cause it was dark, and if it was a book, how could you read in the dark?" He scratches his chin like he's thinking hard about it. While I stand here, completely mesmerized by his words.

"When the guys would all make frozen pizzas in the oven for game night, you'd always make homemade nachos, with shredded pepperjack cheese. I thought that was gross. You had a pet frog named Lucille," he continues.

"Clarke …" I blush and look down.

"I didn't know how to talk to you, but you always fascinated me," he states, gently lifting my chin and making eye contact.

I smile sarcastically. "By my strangeness?"

"No." He shakes his head, and as if in slow motion, his eyes dip to my lips and then back to my eyes.

My nerves are frayed. Crushes are fun because most of my life, they have been fictional. I've never had a guy pay attention to me like this. I mean sure, he has kissed me before, at the Bean. But that was just part of the game—our rouse.

It would kill him to know that our kiss that day was my first. I'm thirty-one and have never been kissed, and no, that fact is not as romantic as the Drew Barrymore movie. *Well, now I have,* but no, I mean, *really kissed.* I've never been kissed, *for me,* the entomologist who wears Birkenstocks, hates basketball, and loves gluten and a good Zach Bryan song. No one has ever had a crush on me; my feelings have always been one sided. Of course, it scares me to feel real feelings for Clarke because I have opened myself up for another rejection. But now I'm terrified because he's acting like he might feel those things for me too. But how do I know for sure? Where do we go from here? I've never been here before.

"I was fascinated by how someone could be so brilliant, confident in themselves, and … beautiful all rolled into one." He brushes a piece of hair behind my ear.

"I'm not sure we're talking about the same girl." I shamefully look away.

"Oh, I'm certain I am," he says. Reaching out his hand, he daringly places it along my waist.

He leans his other arm against the oak tree. He towers over me, and my heart hammers in my chest. Can he hear it?

"You don't seem so bad at talking now." I grin, looking up at him. My cheeks feel hot, and my nerves get the best of me. I tug on his arm. "Come here, I'll show you."

"What?" he asks, dropping his arm from my waist.

Chapter 18

"Climb the tree, follow me." I lift my foot onto the bottom branch and climb up the tree.

He follows behind me.

I get high enough for my thirty-one-year-old self—I'm not as fearless as I used to be. Clarke sits opposite me on the branch, dangling his legs off either side.

"I did climb the tree to read by the moonlight, but also ..." I point up, and he follows my finger up, and his jaw drops open.

Stars.

Constellations.

"It was dark enough to see them, and you can barely see them anywhere else in the city." My heart relaxes a bit with the distance between us. But I take this moment as he stares up at the sky to trace my eyes along the shadows of his biceps peeking out of his T-shirt and at his angular jawline. I bite my lip as his eyes land on mine again.

"Thanks for sharing this with me." He nods and offers a genuine smile. That's not to say that all his smiles aren't.

"Ready to go home?" I ask him, scared of what else could transpire between us tonight. Best case, we could kiss. Worst case, I could be misreading all these signals and signs. Grandma Irene thought I had a boyfriend before, but in truth, Peter never talked to me outside of Tinder.

I just don't want to ruin things.

Chapter 19

"You are in so. Much. Trouble." Sara sprays me with the water hose at the garden; she's helping me with some chores.

"Hey, if you don't quit, I'm going to go turn on the purple hose, and that one only sprays on the stream feature!" I point at her.

"Hey, that one hurts!" Sara shouts over at me and redirects the water onto the roses.

"That's what I thought." I smugly grin and check the roses for pests. I carry a little container with me, eager to see what critters I'll find on the leaves.

"How is your research going?" Sara asks me.

I blow out a sigh.

"What?" she responds.

"It's not. I mean, I'm still in the funding process." I use tweezers to pick a little aphid off the leaf. I set him free in my container.

"Well, that seems to be going really well. You just opened

three weeks ago, and so many roses have sold, pretty soon there won't be any left to pick." She voices one of my biggest fears. I mean, for this season it's fine. We'll close the garden up for the season in just two weeks. But the hype was so large, what if it was too large? What happens when there aren't any roses left to pick next season? Will people still come for their picture under the rose arch? Buy into the love luck scheme?

"How much did you make this week?" Sara asks. Some may consider this way too personal of a question, but it doesn't bother me, not with Sara.

"We made just over a thousand dollars." My eyes widen, and I glance in her direction and smile.

"What?!" she gasps, and suddenly I feel a cool splash of water on my arm.

"Hey, you!" I shout at her and walk over to the purple hose attached to the pink barn.

"No, no, no, Rosie! No!" Sara squeals.

"Too late! It's on!" I twist the nozzle, and a blast of cool water streams out of the hose. She is lucky she's hiding behind the roses, and I am not spraying this guy toward that gorgeous bunch.

"Just put the hose down; we can talk about this!" Sara dramatically shouts.

I just shake my head and laugh at her.

"How much does the research project cost overall?" she asks as I spray the bird poop off the pink barn.

"It's about twenty-two thousand," I say over my shoulder.

"And how many fellow entomologists are contributing?"

"Five others," I say.

"So twenty-two thousand divided by five?" Sara says that like that makes the total sum so much easier and more attainable.

"Uh-huh, do the math, S," I yell back at her.

"Okay, hey now, Rosie, that's only four thousand and four hundred dollars on your tab." I see her smile, and it makes me happy that she's so interested.

"True, but I don't think I can keep up a thousand dollars a week here, plus half of my earnings go to my grandparents for a little while, and the cost of putting money back into the garden as well. It's this business mess that I am not used to as an insect scientist." I sigh and shrug. She walks closer to me, and I reach down to turn off the purple hose, but not without one little …

"Ouch! Rosalie St. Clair! That hurt!" Sara jumps and runs back behind the roses again.

"I had to get you back; it's only fair." I turn off the purple hose.

***

A few hours later, we are lying down on the welcome bridge.

"So," Sara says, and I know what's coming. I'm honestly shocked she hasn't brought it up before now.

"What do you remember about Washington in high school? I remember out of all your brother's guy friends, Washington was the only one who ever referred to you as Rosie. The other ones just called you little sister." That is some interesting memory of hers, as I do not remember that.

"I remember he transferred to the school our freshman year, but he was a sophomore," I say, looking up at the blue sky. It's a super sunny day; I should have sunglasses.

"Oh yeah, he was a transfer. Where did he move from?" Sara asks me, but I furrow my brow. I don't actually remember. Or maybe it never came up. I remember what he said the other night about Naperville not being his hometown. So, I wonder where it was?

"I remember that the Fields adopted him, right? I think I maybe went to that celebration dinner at my church in 2008," Sara thinks aloud.

I didn't expect our little conversation to take such a plot twist. He was adopted? As a teenager? I'm not sure why I never realized this before. I guess I just wasn't paying attention. My curiosity is piqued. I want to hear more of his story; I want to know everything he is willing to share.

"Wanna go get Pho?" Sara asks, breaking me from my thoughts.

"Sure, but then after, I'm going to his first preseason basketball game." I sit up on the welcome bridge and scratch my back.

"Rosie, have you talked to your fam about this dating you're doing?" Sara asks, and I glare at her.

"What do you think?"

"You guys are all over social media. Love in Bloom is busy, and there are always people recording," she explains to me.

"That's kind of creepy," I tell her.

"Yeah, it is. What is up with people these days? Like enjoy your own lives and stop stalking others!" she says.

"Exactly!" I loudly agree with her.

"Except, I suppose paparazzi has always existed. Do you remember that song?" she asks me, laughing and bobbing her head.

"No! Don't start singing it! It will get stuck in my head," I tell her and plug my ears.

"Okay, new topic. What are you wearing tonight?" Sara asks.

"I don't know." Because honestly, I have no idea.

"You should wear his jersey," Sara states without a doubt.

"What?" I gape at her. "I ... I don't know, girl, I ...," is all that comes out of my mouth. My cheeks are heating up again, and it's not just the sunshine.

"You like him, don't you? You said you do, so don't deny it now," she corners me.

"Yes, yes I do," I admit, biting my lip.

"Well, you should! I bet he would like that." She smiles big and lays her hand on my knee.

"But—" I begin, but she cuts me off.

"Enough with the buts tonight. But nothing." She shakes her head and looks at me.

"Who is taking you? You can't take a ride-share to downtown," she asks, voice filled with concern.

"One of the team wives is taking me. She lives pretty close to me. Her name is Mandy Maxwell."

"Oh right, the nice one at that practice." She nods her head and pats my knee.

"They were all nice, in their own way," I say, unconvincing.

"Mm-hmm, keep telling yourself that. Well, let's get going; we have two stops to make," she says.

"Two? Pho and?" I ask her, brows furrowed.

"Wear his jersey, girl. Trust me." She winks at me, and I blush.

"Fine, yes, okay, we will also stop at the Sports Wear store. I just hope they have his number," I say, trying to conjure some of that same *doting girlfriend energy* I showed before at his practice.

How do I get brave again? Because tonight, well, tonight I'm nervous. But tonight is different; tonight I've acknowledged that I've totally and completely caught feelings for number eighteen.

Chapter 20

I'm walking into the arena, arm in arm with Mandy, Ace's wife. I texted her and ended up bringing the jersey to her house to get ready. Her style is much different than mine, and she asked to give me a makeover. I couldn't say no. But my oh my, I don't recognize my reflection. She fixed my hair, so my platinum waves are in two small buns atop my head. She let me borrow some gold hoop earrings and told me to wear high waisted biker shorts with the jersey. I sat in her bathroom, and she did my makeup for twenty minutes. I was a little nervous that Clarke wouldn't even recognize me. Heck, I was a little nervous that I wouldn't recognize me. I never wear this much makeup. I'm a bug girl, for goodness' sake.

As I looked into the mirror, I realized she really only gave me a deeper color lipstick and thicker eyeliner—not too bad. The jersey is oversized—it goes down to my thighs, almost like a dress. A super short dress, more of a reason to wear the biker shorts too. Though I asked if I could wear yoga pants, and she replied, "What, are you crazy?" So I guess that was out of the question. She gave me some knee-high boots to wear, which made me feel a little off my rocker. I insisted that I could just wear my white Converse instead. I hoped I wasn't hurting her feelings, but there was no way I could get around in those heels. She accepted my compromise. Her last move was to spray me down with Eternity by Calvin Klein. I coughed, but figured I smelled pretty good, better than I do on most dates, *erm*, hang outs with Clarke.

And now, as I walk into the arena with Mandy, I'm reminded he probably won't even see me tonight. I told him I was coming, but he's got to focus, so again, I doubt I will see him. I feel self-conscious; I look so different. I feel … trendy? Maybe? I'm not sure what one would call this look.

"There's the ladies' section! Hey, Gianna! Look who I got!" Mandy pulls me onto the court, and my heart nearly stops. We're sitting courtside? That shouldn't be allowed. Won't that be more distracting?

"Shouldn't we be up in a box or something?" I slowly spin around, taking in the arena. There is confetti, loud music, and an announcer. I figured this would only happen during the season, not preseason games. But lo and behold, I was very wrong.

I was also very wrong by thinking I wouldn't see Clarke. Because there he is, running plays with his other teammates.

"Come on, girl, sit next to me, right on the end." Mandy sets her hand down on one of the floor seats. I gulp and slowly sit down.

"It's pretty packed for a preseason game," I say to Mandy.

"What did you expect? All the true fans are stoked for the season to start! So there are tons of people here gearing up for the season. Plus, girl, the tickets are a little cheaper during preseason," she explains.

"Ah." I nod my head and sit down, trying to figure out how to position my legs. If I cross them, the jersey will ride up, and while I'm wearing shorts, that still feels odd. I try and think of the Princess Mia posture on *Princess Diaries*, but that is equally uncomfortable.

The music starts bumping, and I decide knees touching, just right out in front of me is as acceptable and comfortable as I'm going to get.

"Here they come! And it's Thursday! You know what that means, ladies!" Gianna shouts and claps, so I clap along too. I barely notice how the rest of the ladies pull out compact mirrors, and how they are suddenly puckering their lips in their mirrors and/or applying Chapstick. *Odd.*

"Dusk Till Dawn" by Zayn and Sia starts playing full blast on the speakers. I'm super tempted to cover my ears, but I try my best to shake it off and just be cool.

The guys, so stinkin tall, all of them, run past us. A few stop, laughing, and they look up at the Jumbotron. Gianna's husband walks over to her and gives her a big kiss. It takes me by surprise, so I clap just as much as the audience does. They roar and whistle from above in the stands. Then number thirteen approaches his girlfriend and does the same thing.

My stomach drops.

Wait.

Kiss Cam?

Dread hits me as I slowly glance up to the Jumbotron. The camera zooms in on Clarke and another teammate. The other teammate points over his shoulder, and I'm trying to make out his words to Clarke.

Birkenstocks? I lower my head for a moment, to mouth the

word he just said, and my eyebrows fly to my forehead in realization.

Me.

As I lift my head, sure enough, Clarke fills my space. His eyes dip to my lips, just as they did the other night. For a moment, it feels like it's just us. But it's not—we're surrounded by hundreds of people, if not more.

"Kiss! Kiss! Kiss!" the audience chants.

His palm slides around my cheek, and he pulls my lips to his. His other hand finds mine and gives it a squeeze. It's a quick kiss, just for the cameras. As he backs up from me, he looks stunned. But I can guarantee it's not as much as I feel. My lips part; I want him to come back so we can continue that pillowy soft kiss. But the problem is, I'm not sure if that was for real or just for show.

He runs backwards and nods to me, smiling. I smile back at him.

Doting girlfriend? Check.

Confused Rosalie St. Clair? Check.

I've now had two kisses. But I don't know, I still wouldn't consider either one of them as my first kiss. And I don't know, maybe that's cheating. But I'm talking about a first kiss for Rosie St. Clair in the flesh, fully bugged out.

Not Rosie at the Bean, being kissed to throw off paparazzi, or Rosie at the basketball game on the Kiss Cam.

But just Rosie being kissed for being Rosie.

Yes, I'm thinking in third person, and I need to quit it.

The game starts, and my eyes are directed to the court. The girls clap and some shout for their men. I'm enthralled by the game and how they play. Particularly Clarke. He's really good. And we're seated so close, this is pretty cool.

112

Chapter 20

At one point, I stand and whistle for Clarke after he makes a basket.

And soon I'm on my feet after every call involving him. The ladies glance up at me after I stand to yell at the ref during a foul play.

That's when I realize yeah, *I got it bad.*

Chapter 21

The group of us girls are dismissed by security after the guys run off the court. They won the game, and the hype is real. Who knew I *could* actually enjoy a basketball game?

"You riding home with Clarke, I assume? You can pick up your car tomorrow," Mandy asks me in her New Jersey accent.

"Yes, I believe that's the plan, and perfect, thanks." I nod to her and smile. "Thanks for everything tonight. I'll return your things to you next time I see you."

"Okay, baby girl, take care." She pats my shoulder and walks down the opposite hall.

"Come on, sweetie, locker rooms are back this way," Gianna tells me as I'm sure I look like a fish out of water.

"Oh, okay, thanks!" I exclaim and follow her down a dim hallway.

I check my watch, no texts. I tap my foot, just trying to pass time. It's been about thirty minutes. But I suppose after the coach talk, showers, and teammate banter, thirty minutes sounds about right.

Finally, the locker room door opens, and a whoosh of cologne and sweat penetrates my nostrils.

As if in slow motion, Clarke walks over to me with his special swagger. He's got his black athletic blazer on. He smiles at me—well a type of smolder actually. One that I've never seen him possess. He grabs hold of my hand like that's his only job, and whispers, "Let's get out of here."

I lean into him and look down, heart hammering in my chest once more. Are we about to become more? Like a real couple? I'm all in. I just need him to take the lead, but after tonight, I think this is it. This could be it.

Once we get to the stairwell, he laughs, "Rosie St. Clair, you seemed to really be enjoying yourself out there tonight. I've never seen you enjoy basketball."

I giggle but stay silent.

"And silence … and, and so much makeup. Don't tell me, Mandy got a hold of you?" He chuckles, still holding tight onto my hand, guiding me down the staircase to the parking garage.

"Why is there so much silence though? Is something wrong?" We reach a landing on a level in the parking garage that's mostly cleared out. There is no one else but three parked cars around, so I suppose I can try and find my voice.

"Clarke …" I look up at him, my voice coming out a bit too breathlessly. Maybe he will take it like I'm out of shape from these stairs, but as he leans in closer and closer, and my back meets the concrete wall, my eyes search his in this stairwell.

"I didn't really plan to do this here, but …" He leans in, slips his hand around my neck, and brushes his thumb against my jaw. My body is set on fire by his touch, and by the fact that this isn't for paparazzi—it's just us. I think this could be it. The moment. Our moment. I part my lips as he dips his head. He tilts up my chin, and as our lips are about to meet, I hear a familiar voice that makes me feel sick to my stomach.

"I had to come down here myself to see it. Brock Keller texted me—heck, even Roxy texted me. I see why you've been avoiding the family group chat, Rosalie," my brother's rough voice cuts through the air. Clarke backs up from me, but I hold onto his hand and don't let go as we walk to face Ryder.

"Ryder," Clarke clears his throat, addressing my brother. He takes a step toward him.

Ryder's standing by his blue Jeep, on this particular parking landing—*of course he is*. Of course we would run into him.

He's angry. Understandably.

"You came back to town, why? Stay in your own city! Why come back to Naperville? Heck, find a girl in your city, right here!" he shouts at Clarke, widening his arms. "But my sister? How dare you? How dare you? Who do you think you are?" Ryder has always been shorter, but he's super buff. He approaches Clarke, getting closer and closer.

I'm still holding onto Clarke's hand. I'm standing just off to his side. I move my other hand to his as well; I grip his wrist as his chest heaves up and down.

"Clarke," I whisper to him.

"Shut up!" Ryder screams at me.

I back up, and my heart shuts up as well. *Ow.*

"Hey!" Clarke yells at him, taking a step closer to him and farther from me.

"Why are you pretending? Don't kid yourself. You and I both know you'll just hurt her. You'll ghost her just like you did me!" Ryder shouts, hitting his chest like he's looking for a fight. It's a bit surprising to me that Ryder can keep such good composure

116

in the courtroom—he's always been a hothead.

I watch Clarke's jaw; it's clenched. His grip on my hand tightens, but then one moment later, it loosens, and he drops my hand.

No.

"Ry! Stop!" My voice is laced with pain. That small move by Clarke just now feels like a dagger to my heart. That may be dramatic, but when it's rejection number four hundred, any trace of it doesn't just sting—it breaks me. I finally have someone in my life who I think is capable of loving me for me, and my family is driving him away too.

"I forbid you to see him." Ryder looks at me, his eyes drilling through mine with anger. I stand just between them, off to the side, in a triangle. Taxis begin driving down from the levels above us, passing us. People are witnessing this terrible scene.

Why must it always crash and burn? I still try to maintain composure.

"Ry? What are you talking about? I'm a grown woman, and besides, we're friends." I talk with my hands and point between us.

"You're betraying me, Rosalie! Just like he did!" he shouts, pointing between all of us.

"Stop, no, you don't understand." I pause, weighing my choice to tell him about the ruse.

But is it a ruse anymore? I've gone and fallen for someone who is the complete opposite of me—someone who, in my family's eyes, is forbidden by his past betrayal. Could we ever seriously be together? With what we both do? A bug research scientist and a professional basketball player?

"Just friends, says the girl wearing *his* jersey." Ryder's voice reeks of sarcasm as he spits on the cement. "How did this happen? You two are from two different worlds." Ryder laughs, and his voice turns spiteful. "If you saw her bug collection, it would scare you away."

I step backwards, taking a vocal punch to the heart from my brother. *I'll always be the weird girl.*

Clarke lunges for Ryder. "You want to punch me, Ryder? Get it out of your system. But leave her out of this. This is between you and me, bro." He points his finger into Ryder's chest and then his own.

"No," Ryder gets in his face, "you don't get to call me bro!"

I step back. I'm done. I can't do this.

I whistle down one of the taxis exiting the arena and jump in. I give them the address of the University Research Center. It's late at night, but the Research Center is open all hours. Some of us think best late at night. Usually that's not me, but there's no way I'm going home to drown myself with matters of the heart.

Lymantria dispar, I'm yours tonight.

118

Chapter 22

～ၐၜၐ～

S even a.m., waking up and stretching. Ah, my neck is sore. I sat on the lab chair measuring moths for hours, taking notes in my journal. My watch died shortly after arriving to the Research Center. The taxi was a bit expensive, but I would have paid anything to get out of there. I didn't feel like being the butt of any more jokes or comments that I usually subject myself to with my family. So I escaped. And Clarke, well, I have no idea where I stand with him. The logical side of my brain tells me that he let go of my hand to protect me since Ryder's anger was escalating. But my heart tells me that he doesn't want the drama, and now being with me means loads of drama. I'm not sure if he will think the weird bug girl is worth it. I yawn, picking up my head off my crossed arms. I squint as sunlight peaks through the blinds, and I spy out the window that the trees are finally changing colors. The mixed hues of red, yellow, and brown on the campus are beautiful. I suppose I should turn on my phone and ask Sara for a ride home. After I need a ride to go get my car from Mandy's, but first I need a shower. I don't want Mandy seeing me like this. I'm already sick about the drama. I don't want anyone else to know.

It is a Saturday, so Sara should be off work.

As my phone screen tells me, "Good morning," I gasp at all the text messages popping up on my home screen. I always turn my phone off in the research lab to focus, but oh my, now I feel bad.

Clarke: rosie, are u okay?

Clarke: will you just let me know that ur safe?

Clarke: did you get home ok?

Sara: Rosalie, hey, Clarke told me you guys had a rough night and you had to take a taxi from downtown. Can you call me? We just want to make sure you are safe. Plus, I want alllllll the details. That is, if you wanna talk.

Sara: Rosie Elizabeth. Seriously, come on girl. Here, I'll give you an out, just text: Y and I'll know you are okay.

Clarke: i'm so worried about you rosie, pls text me.

Sara: Okay, so last call homegirl. I'm about to call your mom. Yes, I still have her number memorized from childhood. Does she still have you on her FindMe app? Actually no, I hope not; that would be creepy. But, also, I really hope we find you soon. Love you.

Mom: Rosalie, your friends are worried about you and now we are too. Can you please call me and tell me where you are?

Dad: *Six Missed Calls*

Clarke: praying

Oh my gosh! I feel so bad! I scramble to open my phone and click to call Sara. Man, is she going to be mad.

"Rosie? Are you okay? Oh my goodness, we've all been so

worried!" Her voice floods with relief. I hear some people in the background, *"Oh thank God!"*

"I'm okay, I'm so sorry for making you worry. I'm at the Research Center."

"She's okay, she's okay!" Sara tells the people in the background.

"Where are you?" I ask her.

"I've been at your parents' house all night. You are lucky; me and your parents were *this* close calling the police." She emphasizes *this.*

I shake my head. I'm so mortified with myself. So embarrassed.

"I need you to come get me and take me home." I sigh.

"Rough night?" she whispers into the speaker.

"Yep, I'm going to go pick her up. Yes, I'll bring her over later, I promise," Sara tells my parents.

"How about I just tell you all about it when you get here?" I answer Sara's question.

"Sounds good; on my way," she says.

"Thanks, S," I say, tearing up a bit.

"Anything for you, girl; so, so thankful you are safe. Are you going to text Clarke, or should I?" she asks—a true friend. Willing to do my dirty work.

"I got this, thanks, S. I'll see you soon." She says bye, and we hang up.

***

Sara picks me up in her red Honda civic, and all I can do at first is yawn.

"Tell me about it," she says.

"Oh right, sorry. I bet you are even more tired than me. Staying up all night? Are you crazy?"

"Ma'am, I wasn't referring to your yawn. Tell me about what happened last night. Walk me through it; how did you get to the Research Center?" she asks, but I know that she must know a little bit from Clarke.

"What did he tell you?" I wonder aloud.

"He DM'd me around eleven thirty. Said he had been driving around looking for you for an hour and that you wouldn't answer your phone."

"Oh, Clarke," I sadly sigh. I feel so bad.

"But he didn't really tell me what happened, just that you were upset, and he needed my help." She glances at me.

"We were at the basketball game," I begin, cracking a bit of a smile. "I was actually having a good time with the ladies. There was a Kiss Cam …" I swallow hard, knowing Sara is going to want details on that.

"I want details on that," she confirms my suspicion.

"I know, in a minute." I grin at the memory. "I cheered for him, he played great. And the whole game, I couldn't stop thinking about dating him for real. I've been so scared to act on any signals or signs—you know how I am," I explain myself.

"Oh, yes," she says.

"Well, I was too afraid to confront him and offer my feelings. But I promised myself that if he led us towards dating for real, or I don't know, if he tried to kiss me? I would kiss him back," I ramble.

"But he did kiss you?" Sara says.

"Well yes, but that wasn't just me. That was for the basketball audience. I mean, come on, that was for show."

"Or maybe he's just trying to show you off?" she suggests.

"There's no way to know which it is, though." I shrug.

"Oh, Rosie."

122

"I know, S, I know. I'm too scared of rejection. I know." I cast my eyes to the side.

"Okay, then what happened?" she eagerly asks.

"I waited for him near the locker rooms, after his game. He came out, and I had never seen that look in his eye before. So settled, like resolve. Almost like he made up his mind about something, and I hoped that it was us."

"Okay, and?" she questions me, hopeful.

"Then he led me down the stairs of the parking garage and was flirting, at least that's the signal I got." I smile at the memory.

"Oof, did you read the signal wrong? Is that when he rejected you?" she asks, jumping ahead.

"No, he uh, we uh, we almost kissed in the stairwell." I look out the window, and she slams on her breaks at a stop sign. In the mirror, I watch my cheeks turn bright red.

"Rosalie Elizabeth! Then what happened? What's the problem? Why didn't you call him?" she shouts.

"Hey now, my phone was turned off. It was an accident!" I exclaim.

"Okay, but why on earth were you at the Research Center and not watching a movie in his loving arms last night?" She eyes me.

I take a deep breath and sigh once again before I deliver my answer.

"Ryder."

"Ryder?" she asks.

"Yep, he was there, S. In the parking garage. He called us out. He saw everything."

"That little stalker." She slaps her leg while keeping her other hand on the steering wheel. Her reaction makes me laugh.

"He said he saw the social media posts from friends and that Roxy texted him too."

"That little stink!" Sara shouts.

"Yeah, yeah okay, calm down. I've met all my quota of shouting for the next year."

"Yikes, so it was bad?" She checks her rearview mirror and changes lanes.

"Oh yeah, it was bad. He was calling Clarke out for the past and for his betrayal. Then he accused him of using me just to move on and leave. None of which I think are true. I stood there with him for a while, holding his hand. But then Ry got worse and worse. Ryder screamed at me to shut up when I tried to talk to Clarke."

"Ryder James ... Ryder James, just shameful." She shakes her head.

"Yeah, it wasn't fun. Then he started with his sarcasm, and you know ..." I shrug, tears touching my eyes again. I wish it didn't matter, what he says about me. What my family thinks.

"Ryder can get mean when he's sarcastic," she agrees.

"Yep, and he did. He threw me and my bugs under the bus." I wipe away a lone tear.

She cringes. "Aw man, Rosie, I'm sorry, girl. I hate how your fam can't see all the good you're doing for the world in your field of work. Plus, what an amazing person you are in addition."

"I just don't fit in with them, and I never have." I swipe another tear from my eyes. "Isn't it silly, S? I'm still crying about this at age thirty-one." I laugh at myself.

"Don't laugh, Rosie; it's something that hurts your heart. So you should give it space to hurt. Don't shame yourself. It's a hurtful thing. I'm sorry your family can't see you how Clarke and I do." She sneaks that last part in.

"Well, I don't know, Sara. He let my hand go last night. He didn't try and get me to stay."

"Girl, he was probably just trying to keep you safe. He was probably relieved that you left away from a volatile Ryder. Plus, he may not have begged you to stay, but he did do something that we love watching in the movies." She smirks.

"And what's that?" I ask her, arms crossed.

"He ran after you," she states that fact.

I nod slowly, acknowledging the truth in her statement.

"Give it another go, girl. Call him when you get upstairs. Don't delay; he's worried sick." She grabs my shoulder as she puts her car in park at my apartment complex.

"Yeah, good idea. I'll do that. Thank you, girl, love you so much." I reach out and hug her neck.

"Love you. And, Rosie, focus on the real. Don't get too caught up in your fear of rejection. Give yourself permission to expect the best and not just the worst. 'Kay?" Sara holds onto my hand before I step out of the car.

"Okay, yeah. You're right. Thanks, S. I'll call you in a little while to go get my car." I nod, exiting the car, still clad in my clothes from last night. Though one bun is now haphazard, leaning down on the side of my head like Princess Leia.

As I climb the stairs, I dig in my fanny pack for my key. Sometimes the weight of rejection feels so heavy, it feels like everyone knows. Everyone can see your insecurities, like it's written across your forehead. But I glance down at the apartment below mine, Mrs. Kraft and her dog, Jinky's. If they saw me right now, she would see the last name Washington on the back of this jersey and the number eighteen, and you know what? She probably wouldn't think anything of it. She is a caring old lady with her own life moving forward. Her sole focus isn't me and my love life. The world does not revolve me, and thank God for that. This is probably another reason that I don't love social media. I don't want to be under a microscope like my poor moths.

I get to the final step and gasp as I reach out to unlock my door.

There, on my doorstep, lays a very tall, very scrunched up, six-foot-seven, African American, very handsome basketball player, with his mouth hanging open, fast asleep against my door, holding a bag of takeout.

Oh, Clarke.

Chapter 23

"Clarke," I whisper. It is still pretty early in the morning, and I don't want to wake the neighbors. "Clarke," I whisper again, kicking his shoe a bit with mine.

He startles and shoots right up. "Rosie?" He blinks.

I lower to his level and reach out my arms, wrapping his neck in a hug.

"I'm so sorry I scared you. I'm okay. I'm okay," I whisper in his ear as I hold him tight.

He wraps his arms around my middle. "I'm so glad you are safe. I was so worried."

"I know, I'm so sorry. My phone was off. I went to the Research Center after everything."

"You were upset." It's not a question but a statement. I nod to answer him. I pull back from him, just a bit to explain.

"But I didn't mean to not answer you or Sara or my parents. I always turn my phone off in the lab, and then I fell asleep. I'm so sorry for scaring you. What are you doing here?" I ask him as he sits on my bumblebee welcome mat.

"I drove around looking for you for hours. I wasn't in a great space. So I stopped by your Boba café—surprisingly, it was open until midnight. I ordered some Boba and also some Thai food at the place attached. Figured I would come back here and wait for you to get home."

"Did you think I'd be able to smell that Thai food? Because I have to admit even at seven in the morning, six hours later, I'll confess, the smell is not repulsive." I chuckle, trying to lighten the mood a little.

"I was so worried about you." He holds my face in his palms, and for a moment, I think maybe this, maybe this is our moment. *Now.* Finally.

But his phone alarm goes off. He shuts his eyes and drops his hands to grab at his phone.

"What's up?" I say as he opens his home screen.

"It's my alarm to wake up. I'm going out of town for an away game today."

"Oh, and here I thought we could go get Thai food at eight in the morning." I smirk at him, an easy smile pulling at my lips.

"I wish." He locks the phone and goes to stand. He helps me stand first as I untangle from his lap.

"The game is in Phoenix. I don't think it's going to be televised here."

"Whoa, whoa, whoa, are you expecting me to watch all of your games now and just become obsessed with basketball?" I playfully hit him on the chest.

He smiles. "No, I just know you really enjoyed it yesterday. So, I thought I would pass that along to you." He nudges my shoulder.

I bite my lip for just a second. I can't help but smile because I am totally teasing him, but he's not catching on.

Chapter 23

"What?" he says, leaning in once again, picking up my haphazard bun and letting it flop down. "You look like—" he starts.

"Don't say it; I already know." I shake my head and roll my eyes.

"What? Granola girls don't like *Star Wars*?" He chuckles and crosses his arms in front of him.

I give him a side-eye. "Not this one."

His phone alarm goes off again, reminding him of his other commitment.

"I have to go. Can you throw this away? And promise me you won't try to salvage any of this. I don't want you getting food poisoning." He bends his head to look me in the eye, making sure that I know he's serious.

"I promise I will not eat any of this," I swear to him.

"Good, cause there is more where that came from when I get back. Okay?" He leans in, wrapping his arms around me one more time in a hug.

"Deal," I whisper against his neck.

We break apart, and he steps around me to descend the stairs.

"Hey," I yell out to him.

"Yeah?" he turns and asks.

"Play good." I smile and fiddle with my key in the door.

"Yep." He nods and continues on his way.

I'll see him when he gets back, and then we'll talk more. However, speaking of talking more? Up next; I have to go see my parents. At least Sara gets to come with me, thank God.

Chapter 24

Sara drove me to get my car, and I introduced her to Mandy. We chatted for a little bit, but then I knew it was time to face the inevitable. Time to go see my parents.

"Well look what the wind blew in," I hear Roxy's obnoxious remark as I walk into the foyer, Sara at my side.

"Well that wasn't very nice," I holler back to her. My mom shuffles to the front of the house and hugs my neck.

"Oh, we were so worried!" she tells me.

I hug her back. "Yeah, my bad. Sorry about that. My phone was off."

"I wonder why." My sister has always been a master in the art of passive aggressiveness.

"Because I was in the Research Center and always turn my phone off when I'm working," I say with a huge sarcastic smile on my face. *Grr.*

Roxy sits on the large L-shaped sectional couch. She's got her legs out in front of her on the coffee table. She's munching on popcorn.

"Why are you home from college? Did practice get canceled?" I joke with her from behind the couch.

"Hey, kiddo, glad you are okay. Be nice to your sister; she hurt her ankle, and that's why she's home for a little bit," Dad says, walking past me, patting my shoulder.

"What! Why did no one tell me?" I pull out my phone and scroll down to the family chat. Oh, yep, there it is. Whoops. I guess I *have* been ignoring the family group chat, but it's not because of Clarke. It's because I'm running a business for the first time in my life and, well, and ... yeah, maybe because I'm busy falling in love on the side. Okay, yeah, *yeah.* My bad.

"I'm sorry, Roxy, I should have been more attentive on the group chat. I'm sorry about your ankle, and I'm sorry about my comment," I say, sitting across the couch from her. She blows her bangs out of her face and avoids my eye contact.

She doesn't respond. The fact that I have rendered her speechless is bizarre.

Roxy always has something to say. She's always been my spitfire little sister. She has jet-black hair and is extremely athletic. She's a very fierce girl. Sometimes she low-key scares me. I mean, compared to her? I've got super blonde hair, freckles, fluff, and I wouldn't hurt a fly. Though, that's because I happen to like flies.

Roxy changes the channel on the television, away from women's basketball to men's.

I eye the scoreboard in the corner of the screen; it's Phoenix and the, *oh my*.

"Hey, how did you get this channel?" I interrogate her.

"Dad is subscribed to the executive basketball package. He gets all the preseason games that his heart desires." She side-eyes me and then over to Dad.

"That's right! So I can watch you play! I am signed up for college and pro! Oh, and I have really been enjoying watching that Caitlyn Clark play basketball," Dad says, tossing a piece of popcorn to himself.

"Oh, that's cool," I say nonchalantly.

"Well, thank you guys for looking for me last night. I didn't mean to scare anyone," I say, walking over to the kitchen to snag a few carrot sticks off the island.

"You scared that boy the most," Mom says.

And here it comes.

"Not true, Sharon. I was the most concerned," Dad says.

"Aw really, Dad?" I ask him—we never have moments.

"Well sure, kiddo, not sure what I would do if something ever happened to you." He reaches forward and pulls me in for a side hug.

This feels so odd. So unfamiliar. So, *nice.*

"Thanks, Dad." I return his hug.

"Now, like your mother said, about this boy," he says, leaning over the couch, grabbing another handful of popcorn.

And here it is again.

"Turn it up!" Sara tells Roxy, and she increases the volume on the game.

"It's so crazy seeing him on tv," Roxy breaks her silence.

"What? How? You guys have been watching Chicago play for years. He's been on the team that whole time," I state the obvious.

"I meant, now that he's all connected with you. You're here, my normal sister in our living room with us. And Washington, he is a professional."

"I'm a professional in my job too," I try and defend myself

when everyone in earshot glares at me.

"Fine, yes, I see what you mean." I sigh.

"I can't believe the boys all used to play together with Chicago West traveling team and varsity all together, all the years that Washington lived with the Fields. I remember how excited Tammy Fields was when she became Washington's guardian. She was so excited to have him play with Naperville ISD," Mom says, cutting up cucumbers in the kitchen. "And now Washington is on tv." Mom shakes her head, lost in a bit of memories.

"Wait, so he wasn't adopted?" Sara asks Mom over her shoulder.

"Nope, and now, this is none of my business. But Tammy shared with us that his mother gave up guardianship of him and his brother."

I'm staying silent because my mind is reeling. *His mother gave up her parental rights, and he has a brother?* I am betting there is so much more to the story of the night he left. I feel sad that he never fully trusted us with it all. When he told us we were like his family and treated us as family. But it's not easy for everyone to trust, especially after you have been betrayed by those you love.

Ah, Ryder.

"Ryder never forgave him. That's why I ran to the Research Center last night. Ryder came to the game, saw us together, and blew his stack in the parking garage." I guess I have decided to take the brutally honest road with my family. This doesn't happen often. I don't often share about my life, but then again, I've never really had many stories to share.

"If a mother's intuition says anything, I think Ryder feels more upset that Washington left without saying goodbye. Not that he is on the television, and Ryder's not," Mom says, and then continues, "But that doesn't excuse his behavior toward you, Rosie, and I'm sorry he said the things he did." I look at her and furrow my brow. How does my mom know what Ryder said to me?

Roxy reads my expression. "Ryder called Mom last night when we were looking for you. She let him have it, don't worry." My eyes get teary that my mom defended me.

Roxy continues the conversation, "Ryder shouldn't feel bad. Washington didn't say goodbye to anyone," she says, stuffing more popcorn in her mouth.

My mouth goes dry as I realize what I am about to say. "He said goodbye to me that night."

Everyone looks at me.

"I didn't know he was leaving, leaving. I just thought he was saying goodnight after the party." I put my hands up, trying to explain.

"This is the perfect segway to my next point." My dad moves closer to me.

"Grandma has seen some photos on the internet. She says you two are an item these days." *An item.* "We're not sure it's the best idea for you to get cozy with him." Dad points to Mom.

"Why not? He's a great friend," I insist.

"A friend?" Sara and Roxy say in unison.

I blow out a breath and stand up, talking with my hands once more. "He's a good guy. Don't you remember? He was so close to our family. He had to leave, and he had his reasons," I defend him.

"Honey, I just don't want him to up and leave you with no explanation," Mom says.

"Or what if he gets a contract from another team? There's

talk," Dad says, standing behind the sofa.

"See, he will leave and leave you heart broken." Mom's hands rush to her mouth.

"Mom, it's okay." I walk over to her and lovingly steal a few cucumbers from her cutting board. "Just trust me, I'll be okay," I tell her and everyone else in the room, for that matter.

"Whoop! Your boyfriend just swooshed a free throw in the last eighteen seconds of this quarter!"

"Ironic, since that's his number," I say, thinking aloud and realizing my error.

Roxy clicks her tongue and tosses her head back into the couch. "Oh, she's got it bad."

"Oh yeah, she does," Sara says, glancing over at me and smiling.

"We're going on a walk, girls. There are veggies here on the counter and ice cream in the freezer. You staying the night, Rosie? Sara?" Mom asks us.

Sara and I look at each other and nod in agreement. Why not?

It'll be like one of our old-fashioned sleepovers back in the day.

As Mom and Dad leave the house, Roxy looks over at me. "You like him."

I chew my cheek. "Yeah, I do," I confess.

"You gonna tell him?" she asks.

That seems to be the burning question.

And you know what?

Maybe I will.

Chapter 25

My phone has never kept me up at night. I'm not guilty of much mindless scrolling, and I enjoy my beauty sleep. But tonight, as I lie in my childhood bedroom, I look up at the ceiling and cannot for the life of me get a certain someone out of my mind. From the successful win he had in Phoenix tonight to afterwards playing truth or dare with my sister and best friend. Now that got a little out of hand.

Truth is, I miss him.

I miss him.

So I text him.

Rosie: Congrats! Great game!

Clarke: wait ... how do you know that we won?

Oops, busted.

Rosie: I was at my parents' tonight. My dad was able to get the game, but don't get too excited, I didn't ask them to put it on if that's what you're thinking. ;)

I expect him to make a joke back but instead he texts me back.

Clarke: how did that go?

Rosie: Wasn't awful. I apologized for scaring them last night, and we talked a little bit.

Clarke: bout what?

Rosie: .....

Clarke: *basketball emoji*

Rosie: Ha, a little bit, yes.

Clarke: very nice

Rosie: What are you up to right now?

Clarke: right now?

Rosie: Yeah

Clarke: me and some guys on the team are eating pancakes in the airport, waiting to board. taking a late flight back to chi.

Rosie: Oh, so you'll be back tomorrow?

Clarke: yep, that's the plan. what are you doing tomorrow?

Rosie: Clarke, I'm falling asleep. Text me tomorrow once you're back in town.

Clarke: will do. goodnight rosie, sleep well.

Rosie: Goodnight Clarke, safe travels.

I want so badly to end my last text with a heart, but I hold my thumb back. I growl and roll over on my pillow. I drift into a deep sleep.

***

Waking up, I stretch my arms across my bed. The sheets still have that familiar cotton scent of childhood. It's dark, the sun is just beginning to rise, it's a beautiful view.

I check my phone, not expecting anything as it's only 6:30 a.m.

I have a text from **Clarke, sent at 4:00 am: made it home**

137

safely. can't wait to see your pretty face today.

My breath hitches at *pretty face.*

I stare out my bedroom window for a couple more moments and then make eye contact with that old large oak tree as it blows in the dawn breeze. I close my eyes and smile, gripping my chest. I think of how I was sure of a kiss when we were teens and then how again, just weeks ago, I expected it at my grandparents' property.

It's time.

Chance of getting rejected be damned.

I roll out of bed, slipping my feet into my Birkenstocks. I approach my dresser, hoping I still have some clothes in here. I usually leave some once a year cause you never know when you'll have a stop in at your parents' house.

Ah-ha. An oversized Tweety Bird shirt sits in my drawer. I have no idea where this came from or whose it is. Did Mom give me Roxy's shirt? Or what is this?

I open the third drawer, and there's a pair of pink Sophie shorts—man, these have got to be old. I forgot these existed; no way they will make it over my thighs now. I look over at the floor, spying my overalls on the ground. I suppose I'll be wearing an oversized Tweety Bird shirt with overalls and Birkenstocks. I grab a peach colored scrunchy off my dresser and tie up my hair into a high ponytail. I grab my fanny pack and do something so out of character for my thirty-one-year-old self.

I sneak out my window.

I'm surprised my parents haven't sealed it up by now.

But as soon as I'm out, I realize there is one more thing I need. I crawl back into the room again and tiptoe to Roxy's room. I open her door and try and sneak in, quiet as a mouse.

She groggily speaks, "What are you doing in here?"

"You don't happen to have a basketball, do you?" I whisper. I can't believe she's catching me in the act.

She points to her floor, by her clothes hamper.

"I better see this basketball again," she says, suddenly leaning up onto her elbow. "You going to see him?" She cracks a sleepy smile.

"What's it to ya?" I ask her, meeting her usual tone.

"Mm-hmm," she nods, "I'll cover for ya, as long as you answer texts like a sane person."

"Yep, promise. It's right here fully charged." I thump my phone in my fanny pack.

"Right, well good luck, Tweety." She winks at me and lies back down.

Yeah, yeah. Better this than my sweaty shirt from yesterday.

I put the basketball under my arm and sneak out the window once more.

I walk to a local park, one with a basketball court. I bounce the ball as a soft golden hue engulfs me. The sun rises above nearby buildings and brings the first warmth of day.

Clarke: i'm coming to naperville, what do you want from the coffee shop?

The fact that he guesses I'm awake right now is sweet. I guess I am an early riser.

Rosie: An iced chai latte please, with pumpkin cold foam. Meet me at the 1471 park.

About twenty minutes later, I hear a car door shut just beyond me. I try and shoot my third shot but fail epically. I was foolish to assume I too had this hidden basketball talent that I'm sure my dad always assumed. Truth is, I've never tried before.

I see Clarke, walking with that special swagger of his,

completely unaware of how handsome he is. And to me, that makes him even more attractive.

He arrives holding our drinks, his eyebrows raised. "What are you doing? And what have you done with Rosie?" He chuckles, setting the drinks down on a bench and walking back out to meet me on the court.

"I've been working on my free throw …," I say nonchalantly.

"Oh yeah? At seven in the morning?" he asks. He sounds plenty amused with me.

"Yeah." I nod, trying to act serious.

"Lemme see," he says quietly as he approaches my side, then walks to stand just beneath the basket.

I try my best, sending out a groan at the same time as the ball. He catches it and tosses it back to me.

"Here, here, let me show you. May I?" he asks, approaching me again.

"Sure." I nod.

He moves in to stand behind me. My back presses against his chest, and his strong arms wrap around mine, guiding them to align with the basket. As our skin brushes, the sun casts light on the court, illuminating the shadows. Bravery courses through me, so I shift in his arms and place my hands on his chest. My eyes make their way from his chest to his jaw, and courageously to his eyes. I grip his shirt as I step up on my tiptoes. His eyes search my face as I slowly lean in. I swipe my tongue over my lips and place a feather-light kiss upon his mouth. He responds immediately. Reaching his hand back into my hair and launching his other arm around my waist, he pulls me in, tight against him. His lips, pillow soft, envelope mine in our first real kiss. I move my hand up to his smooth cheek and pull him closer to me. He takes control of the kiss,

140

and I let him lead. As our mouths meet, scorching fire radiates through me. He scoops me off my feet, hands holding my legs around his waist. Which was nice of him, because my calves were burning standing on my tippytoes for so long.

I bring my head back for a second, taking a momentary break from his lips. He reaches forward again, eager to capture my lips again.

I smile at the sight of that.

He wants me.

Just like I equally want him.

"Clarke," I whisper breathlessly.

"Mm …," he moans as his answer.

"I like you."

He leans his head against mine and presses a kiss to the tip of my nose.

"Rosie, I like you too. And hey, you better not refer to yourself as *just* Rosie ever again. You're everything," he captures my lips again. "You're everything," he whispers through our kisses. I wrap my arms around his neck and scoot myself closer to him.

He softly moans into the kisses, and I pull back to nuzzle my nose into his neck. He leans into my touch. I could stay like this with him all day. I want to stay with him all day. He gently sets me back down on the ground. I know soon we'll have some company out here, but it's nice to have this moment. Alone. Real. Without the cameras.

"Are you gonna leave?" I ask; my hands lightly sit on his hips, tracing circles.

"I'm not going anywhere." He pulls my head against his chest and kisses the top of it. "You wanna get out of here?" He holds me.

"I don't really look the part." I look down at my Tweety

ensemble and worry for a moment.

"Says who? I think you look beautiful, Rosie." He tugs on my hand as he picks up our drinks from the bench and guides me to his car.

"I want to take you on our first real date," he confirms, sitting down in the driver's seat, his hand instantly seeking mine out.

Now this, *this feels right.*

Rosie: **Success, first real date day commences. I'm safe with him.**

I'll be back later. Love y'all.

Roxy: You go girl.

Chapter 26

He insists that I wear a blindfold on the way to our date, but I tell him that I'll get car sick if that happens. So we compromise, and I don't wear one. His Lambo drives down the highway into the city, but this time, we don't stop on any side roads. Each mile, the Navy Pier comes closer and closer into view. I reach over and pinch his shoulder.

"Are you taking me to Navy Pier?" I feel giddy.

"Have you ever been?" he asks me.

"No! I have always wanted to though. I've heard the waterfront is beautiful!"

"Oh good, it is! Can't believe you have lived here all your life and never been!"

"Yeah, all our spare time was spent at basketball tournaments." I put on a sarcastic smile for him.

"I see. Well, today is your lucky day. No basketball on the schedule." He grins at me and continues driving downtown to a parking garage.

***

"Wow, Clarke, you may need to pinch me!" He holds my hand as we walk into Navy Pier. There is this ginormous boat called the Windy. The waves crash up against the pier. It's a beautiful overcast October day today. The perfect Chicago weather for a first date day.

"They have a children's museum! How cool!" I point to the museum.

"Except that's for kids, Rosie." He pulls me in the opposite direction, and we window shop instead.

We make little jokes as we walk through the attractions.

"Want some ice cream?" he asks, excited.

"It's only ten in the morning!" I squeal, rocking on my heels.

"So?" he shouts over the people in the line.

"Absolutely! Surprise me!" I holler back and peek around the line. We're drawing a little bit of attention, and maybe we have this whole time, but I haven't noticed. Cause today, we're not here for the paparazzi or anyone else. We're enjoying our time together, finally together for real.

He steps away from the line with two waffle cones, one full of orange sherbet and one with mint chocolate chip. He holds one down to my lips, and I take a lick. *Mmm.* Leave it to Chicago to do a gourmet mint chocolate chip ice cream.

"That is delicious! Taste it," I push it closer to him, and he tilts the orange cone to me. It hits me in the nose, and I snort out in laughter.

"That one is good too, but not in my nose!" He laughs too, apologizing, but I wave him off.

"Do rides make you nauseous?" he asks.

"Surprisingly no. What did you have in mind?" I clasp my hands together and jump in place.

"Man, Rosie, has anyone ever told you that you look adorable when you are excited?" he asks me, leaning in to kiss my cheek.

I shake my head, my ponytail brushing against my neck. "Nope, just you."

He smiles and wraps his arm around me.

We finish the ice cream cones and start walking to the rides.

"Hey, I have an idea." He stops and bends over. I'm flashing back to this moment at the garden.

"A piggyback ride? I thought you were talking about real rides, Clarke!" I laugh, slapping him on the shoulder.

"I am, but your feet look tired, so I just figured I'd be a gentleman, but hey, if you don't want to …" he says, and I shush him and point to the ground.

"Say no more, Washington. I am going to take a rest, and I thank you for your consideration," I joke with him while simultaneously being serious. My feet are tired from all the walking. So I accept the ride.

He lifts me up on his back, and it is in fact like a ride. I can see so much from up here, it makes me giggle. Now I notice people pulling out their phones. But I find that I don't care. I don't care that I have an oversized Tweety Bird shirt on, or that my hair is a mess. I'm just happy to be with him.

He points over to the swings and then over to the merry-go-round.

"Which one?" he tilts his head back to ask me.

"Swings, definitely." I nod and point in their direction.

***

After riding the swings three times over and over, we notice the line has gotten busier.

"So I guess we won't be going a fourth time," he says, grabbing onto my hand again.

"That's okay, let's go on that." I point to the infamous Ferris

145

wheel.

"You got it." He leads me over to the Ferris wheel line.

A few fans approach Clarke and ask for his autograph. He cheerfully obliges. Some kids run up to him, and he gets down on their level to talk, which makes my heart soar. That is adorable.

"Next guests!" says the attendant.

We climb into the seat, and it rocks a bit. I grab hold of his leg quickly, and he wraps his arm around my back, stabilizing me.

"You okay?" he asks.

"Yeah, just a little nervous, I guess. It goes so high up there." My eyes widen as I look up.

"Don't worry, it's just a little taller than me." He smirks, and we both start laughing. I shove him.

"Oh har, har …"

"Really though, don't worry, I promise I'll keep you safe." He tucks me into his arm, and I lean my head against his shoulder. I've never felt this way with anyone. Accepted for who I am. Protected. Cherished like a treasure. I never expected to find this in real life—I thought it only existed in fictional tales. But my heart rate increases the higher and higher we get, and as much as it's because of my nerves, it's equally from my excitement. Just being here with Clarke. In this moment. Everything that has transpired today. It's got me feeling overwhelmed in the best way.

We get to the very top, and it pauses. I tremble a bit. "Hold me tight," I whisper to him, and he scoots in closer to me. He runs his hand down my back, and then plays a bit with my ponytail. Just the scent of his cologne, and the touch of his hand on my back gives me a calming effect.

"Wow, it's beautiful, look!" I say, looking out over Lake Michigan.

"It is," he quietly responds, and I look over at him. He's not looking at the water, but straight at me. *Okay, now this feels straight out of a movie.*

I tilt my head back and lick my lips. I lean back into him and press my open mouth against his. He moves his lips against mine, and it feels absolutely dreamy. His kiss gives me this adrenaline rush. I reach my hand up to cradle his neck and pull him closer as my tongue meets his in this moment of intimacy on the Ferris wheel.

When that realization hits me, that we are indeed in public, I pull away from him.

"Mmm," he sighs.

"Where's the paparazzi?" I mumble.

"Oh, baby girl, I don't need to see any paparazzi to convince me to kiss you." He pulls me back in for a few more lingering kisses. They are sweet and again, pillow soft.

"I can get used to this." I smile; my face feels hot.

He tucks a flyway piece of hair behind my ear and peers into my eyes.

He makes me feel so safe, and because I feel safe, I also feel brave. I see an insect flying just above us and reach out my hands to catch it. As I pull my hands down, I peek at it. It's just a simple June bug. I decide to tell him a secret.

"You know, at youth group when I was a teenager, we would have pool parties. I would scoop these up in the pool and throw them at the girls."

"Rosalie St. Clair, you didn't," he scoffs at me in shock.

"Oh, I so did. It wasn't fair; those girls were so pretty and giggly. They got all the boys' attention. So I took fate into my own hands, threw the bugs in their direction, and they would scream. Then the boys would laugh at them. It made me feel good." I chuckle to myself thinking of the memory. "It was a way I could stand out, and I rocked it," I say confidently, crossing my arms in front of me.

"I have a hard time imagining guys not noticing you in high school. Seriously, hey, they had to be blind." I blush.

"Clarke, you are sweet. But, nope, this is actually my first date ever," I tell him, feeling a bit embarrassed.

"I am honored to be your first." He pulls my hand up to his lips and places a kiss to it.

"It doesn't make you uncomfortable that I'm inexperienced in all this?" I point my finger around us and between us.

"What? Absolutely not. Plus, I'm not experienced either. The media has always gossiped about me, like I'm some single player. But nah, really, I've just never gotten close enough to anyone. I never felt so comfortable and so safe with someone enough to share my life with them. Until you. Knowing you in the past, and having that history, I think that helped a little. But no, Rosie, never be embarrassed with me. We're on the same page, okay?" He looks me in the eyes, and I smile, relieved.

"Plus, you are a great kisser. How'd you manage that?" He nudges my shoulder with his.

"Thirty-one years of dreaming about this moment, maybe?" I giggle, squeezing my face. I'm joking but also, probably not. That honestly probably has something to do with it.

"You've been dreaming about kissing me for thirty-one years? Doesn't that make you ancient?" He laughs, relentlessly teasing me.

"Oh, shut up." I push him, and our seat wiggles, so I cling to him and hold him tight.

He wraps me in his arms, and I just lean against his chest, breathing him in.

"Hey, I have a question," he asks me as we near the bottom of the Ferris wheel. I think it's about time to go.

"Yeah, I could eat. We could stop at that little shack with the hot dogs," I say, clearly thinking about food.

"We can stop there, yeah. But that wasn't my question." He scratches his ear and turns to me.

"Oh, sorry." I grin.

"Well, I guess it's more of an idea. I want to hear your opinion on it, what you think about it?" he says, sort of rambling along. That's my job. Ha.

"Okay, what's up?" I ask him, listening intently.

"I was thinking that tomorrow at Love in Bloom I should fake propose to you. I know tomorrow is the last day before closing up for the season. I want to do something that will leave a lasting impression on people. So when the garden opens next season, there is a line of people at the gate to get in. Would that be weird? But seriously, I think it could get a lot more attention and finish out the season for you really well."

"It wouldn't be weird. That is a great idea. Thanks, Clarke. But also, it wouldn't be weird for you?" I ask him.

"I wouldn't have recommended it if it felt weird to me." He kisses my temple, and we hook arms to exit the Ferris wheel.

"Oh, one more thing before we leave," he says behind me as we walk out of the Ferris wheel. We see a long line of people, a bunch of them waving in his direction.

He surprises me when he spins me into him and dips me down for a kiss.

The crowd hoots, hollers, and whistles. I can only imagine how many phones are out in the crowd, but I am so happy to be his girl.

And I am actually looking forward to sharing this photo with my family and Sara. Not only the photo, but I want to bring Clarke over soon. But I suppose I still need to give each party some time. I just hope it doesn't take too much time to reconnect us all.

I know everyone will forgive him just like I did.

Ryder may take some extra prayers, but I'll get everyone I know right on that.

He flips me back up, and we wave to the crowd. How did I get this lucky? How did I get this blessed?

"Tag, you're it! I'll race you to the hot dog stand!" I press my finger into his chest and take off running.

"Finally, a fair start!" he calls after me.

It doesn't take him long to outrun me, especially because of his super long strides.

I catch my breath right at the hot dog stand, and my eyes catch on the menu.

"Number thirteen: Peanut Butter Dog? Yeah, you are definitely not ordering for me here." I chuckle, locking arms with him.

The best thing is? This is just the beginning. Of us, that is.

Of us.

Chapter 27

As we leave the city, we get stuck in a little bit of standstill traffic on the highway. My head leans back into the seat, enjoying the feeling of the late afternoon breeze.

"You see that exit?" He nods his head to a sign on the highway.

"Yeah, what about it?" My face hurts from smiling, and we haven't even arrived to our date yet.

"That's my hometown," he says.

It catches me off guard. My smile fades, as does his armor. He's being more vulnerable to me. My brows furrow, and I stare out my window, over the railing. The homes in view? Well, I can barely imagine they are in livable condition. Windows are boarded, and doors are gated. Graffiti decorates the alleyways, and trash is piled up in the street.

I take it all in. This is where Clarke grew up. My heart breaks for him as a child. I was right—his story is bigger than any of us know. But now, I have the privilege of learning more.

"Clarke, I, I had no idea …" I reach over and place my hand

against his thigh. His hand covers my hand.

"No one knew, apart from the Fields, of course," he says. His Lambo sits at a standstill on the highway, but I'm thankful for this moment.

"Do you still have family …" I turn toward that side of town to ask him.

"No, they're gone." I look back at him as he makes this admission. He swallows hard, running his fingers across his steering wheel.

"I'm so sorry." My eyes fill with tears. I don't know the whole story, but my heart constricts.

"Thanks," he says, looking forward but then peeking over at me.

"Is it alright if I ask a few more questions?" I tread lightly. I just want to know everything about him.

He works his jaw for a moment, eyes never leaving mine. They look pained. I wonder when he talked about all of this last? Who does he have? Now that his family is gone, Ryder and the guys are gone, and, well, he has his teammates. But are they enough?

"You don't talk about this much, do you?" I brush my fingers along the palm of his hand.

"Never," he chuckles, looking down from me to his lap. He brings our intertwined hands to his lips and kisses mine.

"Ask away; it appears we're stuck here for a little longer." He takes a deep breath.

"Clarke, what are you scared of?" I ask him quietly.

"It's just the memories—they haunt me. My mom, she was beautiful." He smiles thinking of her, and it breaks my heart.

"She was a single mom to my brother and me. Andres was my big brother; we were thick as thieves as kids." He smiles and then sighs, knocking his other hand on the steering wheel.

He chews his cheek and then continues, looking out my window towards his hometown.

"Growing up, we were given two choices: join the gangs or be killed by the gangs. Andres didn't see a way out—heck, neither did I. I always wish I was the older brother, because how things played out for me was so different than how they played out for him. If I had been the older brother, I could have pulled Andres out with me and given him a better life." He blows out a breath.

I move my other hand to rest on his neck, letting him know that I'm right here, coaxing him to go on.

"Mom got a court order to go to this class held at one of the community centers right out of town. Mom was perfect in my young eyes, but she could never stay sober. She brought Andres and I along to the community center, and I started playing basketball. I got pretty good. Long story short," he says as some brake lights start blinking in front of us, suggesting soon we may be able to continue on our way down the highway.

He takes a deep breath. "Long story short, we got invited by one of the community leaders to his church. I wanted to go. Andres, not so much. Mom? She was too gone on Sunday mornings. Andres started taking me until I was old enough to walk there myself. Once Pastor Tom found out I was walking to church, he had the church bus come and pick me up, along with some other kids on my block. Andres fell deeper into the gangs, and by the time I turned fourteen, the court took away my mom's rights to us. Pastor Tom and his wife, Mrs. Lottie, kept up with me at church and at the community center. I was there any time I wasn't at school. I started sneaking in the back door of the church after hours to sleep in the shed on the property. I didn't want to go home. Mom was mentally and emotionally gone, and Andres never came home. One morning, the landscaper found me in the shed and reported me to Pastor Tom. I opened up with him, and he connected me with the Fields. Tammy and Roger volunteered weekly at the community center and had been foster parents for years."

All this information—there is so much of it—sweeps over me in waves. It's all so heavy. I just want to get out of the car and give him a big hug. I want to hold onto him and not let go.

"Like I said, heh, long story short, Pastor Tom and Mrs. Lottie got me connected with the Fields, and they took me into their home in Naperville. You know the rest." He starts to push on the gas, and we move a few feet.

Except I don't know the rest. I sit in this seat, wondering more about his brother and his mom. He started out the story speaking about them in past tense. I'm assuming they passed away, or maybe, maybe he doesn't know. It's heart breaking.

"Clarke, thank you for trusting me with your story."

***

We turn into the rose garden parking lot and decide to go on a walk to my grandparents' property. He has learned to keep bug spray in his car as well. Smart man.

We're walking up through the grassy hill, hand in hand, swaying them between us.

As we reach my grandparents' tree, I reminisce on that graduation night and what he told me a few weeks ago.

"So when you said a few weeks ago that leaving was your ticket out … that night when you left? What did you mean? Didn't your life get better with the Fields?" I ask, turning my head to him.

He nods. "It did, but my junior year, Andres really started

154

messing with me. Andres and the gang wanted me to come join them. I knew right from wrong, and knew I didn't want to join. But the overbearing weight of guilt I felt was unreal. Andres was there when I wasn't. He found Mom, overdosed, the summer before junior year. She was dead. He took care of all of that alone. I didn't even know she passed until December of that year. I felt so much guilt because I was over here playing travel basketball, food on my plate three times a day or more, a roof over my head, people to call friends, and a place to call home. It wasn't fair. I wrestled with it, back and forth. So when Roger came to me, talking about college scouts, I knew that was my only way out. That was my ticket. I rationalized it. I could play basketball, get out, make money, and then come back and save Andres." He looks up at the moon and then back at me. I wrap my arm around his and lean into him.

A moment of silence passes between us, but he blows out a shaky breath and continues, his voice full of emotion, "But I was too late. He got killed, by one of his own. He owed him money. I didn't get to him in time, Rosie." He wraps his arms around me, unable to handle the grief. His chin trembles, and his shoulders cave. He falls to his knees. He leans his head against my stomach, and I just hold him. He weeps.

Clarke's story is so heavy, and to think he carries it around with him every day. To think me and Ryder, heck, my whole family has given him crap over the years for ghosting us.

He got his big break; he escaped.

We're all in the wrong.

But I'm the one who can start to make it right. "Clarke, I'm so sorry. I'm so sorry for your deep loss, and I'm so sorry for only making it harder on you and for thinking for years that you betrayed us. We were the breadcrumbs of this situation," I explain.

"No," he shakes his head, "you guys were everything. It was so hard to leave. I ran away when I got scared. It was too hard," he cries.

He's so hard on himself. I think he did a good job. He thought it out so well, it just didn't go the way he planned.

I kneel in the grass with him and hug his neck, stroking the back of his head.

"Oh, Clarke. You are so strong. I'm so grateful you are in my life. Thank you for coming back."

"It may have started fake, Rosie. But my feelings for you are real. And in truth, even as teenagers, I think it started then. Like I said before, I just didn't know how to articulate it," he explains, wiping his tears away with the backs of his hands.

"Shh, shh, it just wasn't the right timing then, but it is now," I say, leaning in to give him a small kiss.

"Yes, and I thank God every night for that. You are the biggest blessing of my life, Rosie. I mean it." He cups my face with his palms and leans his forehead into mine. We breathe each other in.

"And you are mine," I say.

And he is mine.

Chapter 28

I got a real good morning text this morning. Not a fake one. It was the first one I have ever received as bug-loving Rosie. It makes me smile just thinking back on it. But I can't stay in that memory too long or my mind also tumbles back to what it feels like to be held in Clarke's arms, and that thought is far too distracting to me.

I make sure that I am positioned at the welcome booth this morning so I don't miss his entrance. More and more people shuffle in, but surely, Clarke is so tall, I would have seen him. The girls in the front end up needing help, and so I get into full business mode. I'm a sweaty mess when I realize it's been hours and no Clarke.

I pull out my phone to text him.

Rosie: Hey honey, you didn't get cold feet now, did you? Over our fake proposal? I miss you. Where you at?

I finish my lunch break at the pink barn and check my phone again, no text.

I start feeling a little, just a tiny bit, anxious. I decide to send him another text.

Rosie: Clarke, you okay? Last minute practice?

As the afternoon sun casts on the garden, my heart rate begins to pick up. The fear begins to crawl over my heart, clouding up my mind.

The voices begin: *"He doesn't really want you; you guys were just hanging out; you got too invested; you fell hard, and he did not fall harder; you are such a pathetic thirty-one-year-old; you are too clingy; you will always be the weird girl; he couldn't handle you; he said it himself, it's easier to run when he's scared; he doesn't want you."*

Rejection # I've lost count. I have trouble taking full breaths. I should trust him. I should kick these voices to the curb, but once they invade, it's hard to fight them off. In fact, I don't think they invade anymore. I think they have taken up space in my head for far too many years, and they've turned my heart into their home. Claiming a room for themselves, like a guest that has outstayed their welcome. Though, when does anyone welcome rejection with a smile? Not me, that's for sure.

I thought I was in the clear.

But here it is again, like a tidal wave. *Basketball, guys, grants, family, and now Clarke.*

It's too much.

I take out my phone after I sprint to my car. I breathe heavily, fidgeting with the car door. I get it open, climb in, and try to keep it together. But as I throw the car into reverse, I can't hold it in anymore. My eyes blur, and sobs begin pouring out of me. I slam my hand into my steering wheel. As I turn onto the road, away from any looking eyes, I scream in agony, "Why!"

I click on my Bluetooth and then on Sara's face.

The phone makes that obnoxious noise, and Sara doesn't

pick up. That's probably good. I'm not sure I can form words.

I just don't want to be alone.

My parents are out of town, at a conference.

But Roxy, she might be there.

I just need someone, anyone.

I just want a hug.

***

Pulling up to my parents' house, I'm second-guessing my choice of coming here instead of just going home. Or maybe trying Sara's and just waiting for her to get off work.

Roxy doesn't hug people.

What was I thinking?

I sit in my car, in front of the house. My windows are down. I'm not sure what to say. I'm not sure why I'm here.

"Hey, loser …" I hear a voice and ignore it for a moment, but then I hear it again, and look up. Roxy is standing outside the front door, leaning on the brick column. "Hey, loser!" she yells again. "What are you doing?" This is making me *really* want to get out of the car. Not.

I decide to get it together and wipe my eyes.

I open my car door and try and muster a smile.

"Oh gosh, I'll order the pizza. Come on, extra cheese. On me." She turns and limps back into the house, gesturing that I follow her.

I chuckle, further wiping my eyes, following my little sister into our childhood home.

She sits down on the couch, pulls out her phone, and orders two deep dish pizzas. Her next move shocks me. She reaches for the remote and turns off basketball.

I look at her, dumbfounded.

"Sit down, sis. Tell me what happened," she states.

I sigh, sitting on the couch. "He didn't show up today. We had plans ..." I chuckle thinking about it. "He was going to fake propose to me to increase publicity even more, you know, to close up the season. We had such a good date yesterday. It was so meaningful. *I thought.*"

"Now, Rosie, don't do that. Don't get in your head like that. Did you text him? Maybe something came up? Don't go to the worst-case scenario," she lectures me. I suppose it's better than an "I told you so" speech.

"I did text him. He didn't respond." I shake my head.

"You didn't text any of us last week, all through the night, and it didn't mean that you didn't like him. It didn't mean you were rejecting anyone. Stuff comes up. Something must have come up. You need to cool it," Roxy tells me. While she's right, I am sick and tired of people telling me to calm down, or that I am being dramatic. If she had taken all the rejection over the years, she would struggle with self-doubt too. She's just lucky.

"You don't understand, Rox!" I shout at her.

"I'm sitting here trying, aren't I?" She doesn't raise her voice, just speaks monotone.

In the past, I would think of how insensitive she's being. I would blame her for not understanding me, and I would take it as a personal attack. But for the first time, I really hear her.

She's trying. She doesn't understand me. But she's trying.

She's sitting here with me, ordered a pizza, turned off basketball, and is listening. She is trying. Roxy is a spiky, not touchy/feely creature. How she is behaving right now is out of her element. But she *is* trying. And that doesn't make my behavior defective. My big feelings aren't wrong or shameful. They are part of how I function. They can trip me up, and they can be frustrating, but they've also come in handy as well. Like in the early years, Mom and teachers excessively telling me how compassionate I was. I think these two things connect. And the rejection I've faced over the years, mixed with those things, well, it can make me into a Rubik's cube. Difficult to handle by the average person but treasured by the right ones.

Just like my unique personality, Roxy's got hers too. Blunt to a fault, fiery, fierce, stubborn, extremely athletic, doesn't show emotion easily. But her strengths are also mixed into that as well. She is strong, knows where she stands on issues, a successful athlete, persistent, clever, and loyal. We are different, but there's beauty in accepting that.

"You're right. I'm sorry. I just have a lot of big feelings about this. When we talked the night before, he mentioned he's been known to run when things get hard. What if he thinks this," I move my hand to point inwardly, "is too hard."

"Being with you? Nah." She shakes her head. "That can't be it."

The doorbell rings, and while I know it's the pizza delivery man, I wish it was Clarke.

Roxy pays the man and hops back in with two pizzas and a box of cheese sticks. *Mm.*

"Let's watch a movie," she says, placing the pizzas on the coffee table.

"Shouldn't you be staying off that foot?" I ask her, reaching for the pizza box.

"Well, I didn't see you getting off the couch." She smirks at me and reaches into the box to grab a slice. "What movie do you want to watch?" she asks me.

"What? I get first dibs? Okay, just nothing basketball. I'm not in the mood tonight," I tell her.

"Suit yourself," she says as I move to the kitchen to get us some sparkling waters.

As I turn around, I almost face palm myself.

Remember the Titans.

Well, at least it's not basketball.

Chapter 29

I decide to stay at my parents' for a few days with Roxy. I mean, I go home to feed my critters and get my things. But then I keep coming back each night. It's been three days, and I haven't heard from Clarke.

Even Roxy by now has expressed her dismay and disappointment with him. I'm lying on the loft couch, building up my recipe Pinterest board. I see Ryder's face cross my home screen, and I send his call to voicemail. He is the last person I want to talk to. I can just hear his lecture now. He calls again, and once again, I send him to voicemail. I'm not in the mood for I told you so.

"Oh my gosh, Rosie! Get in here!" Roxy screams from downstairs. Roxy doesn't scream, ever. *What is going on?* My heart reels for a moment as I jump off the couch and head to the stairs. I rush down them so quickly that I'm winded by the time I manage to get to her.

"What?" I look at her, and then my jaw drops as I see the breaking news on tv. Roxy reaches out to hold my hand. I look down at my phone; it's vibrating. Ryder is calling me again. I swipe to answer and lift the phone to my ear, but then I figure, I can't do this alone. So I put the phone on speaker.

"Rosie? You there?" Ryder says with an out-of-character soft voice. "Clarke's in trouble," he says.

The breaking sports news seems to suggest that as well, claiming Clarke Washington has been missing in action to their last two games.

"So, he didn't leave me," I whisper. I should instantly ask what's wrong, but first I have to calm my heart, speak that truth.

"Not yet." Ryder blows out a shaky breath.

"What? What are you talking about, Ryder?" Roxy shouts at Ryder. She takes it upon herself to get it out of him. I nod to thank her.

"Rosie, Clarke was attacked. Found in his apartment, unresponsive three days ago. His place was ransacked."

"Oh my gosh." My heart drops.

"Is he okay?" both Roxy and I say in unison.

"He's at St Joseph's hospital. He's in critical condition. I can come pick you up if you want."

Something is still fishy to me. How does Ryder know all of this? Last time I saw him, he was ready to fight Clarke himself. But his voice now … He sounds afraid, and not guilty afraid but fear birthed from worry, and worry birthed from compassion.

"I need to go to the hospital. I'll drive, but I'll meet you there?" I ask him, as he sounds like he is headed there himself.

"Okay yeah, I'll meet you in the lobby," he says and then hangs up.

Roxy squeezes my hand. "See, he didn't ghost you. In fact, I think he loves you, Rosalie." She gives me a halfhearted smile and shoos me along.

In the next ten minutes, I am out the door, off to the hospital in the pouring rain.

***

I rush into the hospital. I just have to see him. Of course, the rain hasn't let up by the time I arrive at the hospital, and I'm praying that that isn't a sign.

The raindrops drench my hair, so it drips onto the tile in the lobby.

"Rosie!" Ryder calls me over.

He shuffles his windbreaker off his shoulders and wraps me in it. I look at him, my face surely communicating confusion.

Who is this Ryder?

Showing such compassion? For me and for Clarke.

He's holding something in his hand—a thick manila folder.

"Let's go upstairs," he says as he leads me to the elevators. "I'll stay with you for a while. Don't worry, I'm praying he wakes up too."

My brother is being so fake right now. Is it just because once we get in this elevator he has an electrifying "I told you so" speech ready for me?

"Why are you saying this? I know you don't care," I spit fire at him. He has no idea what Clarke has gone through, and his recent run-in with me has left bitterness in my heart.

I watch him clench his jaw, and he looks down, pulling on his suit sleeves. He adjusts his collar, loosening his tie a bit.

"I was wrong," he says.

I'm shocked. Shook. What has gotten into my typical hot-headed brother who became a lawyer because he insists he is always right?

"Come again?" I ask; my eyebrows are just as surprised as I

165

am.

"I was wrong, and don't make me say it again," he says.

Ah, there he is.

"Wrong about what?" I ask. I will enjoy this.

"Thinking he betrayed me," he says nonchalantly. Wait, I thought he was only apologizing for his hurtful words from the game. What does he know?

"What do you know?" I ask him; my curiosity is piqued.

He holds up the manilla folder.

"After our fight, I got this in the mail at my office. Inside, there are news clippings. News clippings about a baby born to Tasha Washington, Clarke, little brother to Andres. Then another, Malik Washington, father to two young boys, dies in drive-by shooting." He sighs. A tear falls from my eye, and I wipe it away.

Ryder continues, "They pulled me in. I never knew about Clarke's origins. Behind the first clippings was a letter from Clarke. He wrote me a letter, telling me everything. He told me about his family, his life before Naperville. His perspective on leaving. How he never wanted to leave his new family, his brothers on the team. He apologized in the letter, sis." Tears continue to fall down my face as my chin trembles.

"Then, after the letter, there was more. He told me about you and him. Your original fake plan." He eyes me, shaking his head. I sadly smile and shrug my shoulders.

"He explained that it was because he wanted me to take his brother's case. He was murdered by an infamous gang leader that runs with some other dangerous guys that the authorities have been trying to put away for years. He thought he collected enough evidence against the guy and would pay me ten times my fee to help get the guy off the streets."

My eyes widen. I had no idea this was going on behind the scenes, yet I guess he did mention in the beginning he needed Ryder's help. And Ryder is a criminal prosecutor.

"I held it all in my hands, weighing the severity. This would be a high-profile case for me, but one with this kind of evidence Clarke had collected over the years ... well, shoot, he had done his part, his own investigation on the side. The perpetrator is definitely wanted for several other murders as well, all over the city and country. I decided to make a few calls." I wipe my eyes again, nodding for him to go on.

"I took the case. I called him four nights ago at the number he left. We discussed how things would begin to shift. I told him since things were in motion, he might be in danger, so to stay extra alert. He told me, well, I should let him tell you what he told me, but in any case, I just told him to be careful with my sister." I choke out a chuckle and slug him in the arm. I'm not going to lie—this is so much more than I expected. I had no idea it ran so deep. I wish Clarke would have let me in on it. But maybe he would have. If he had come to the rose garden that day. Maybe he would have told me that day.

Ryder and I walk off the elevator and take seats in the waiting room.

"You love him, sis?" Ryder asks, leaning onto his knees and looking over at me.

My eyes feel puffy from the tears.

My heart lurches. *Yes.*

"I think that's something I need to tell him first." I smile, turning his words back to him. Assuming that Clarke did indeed tell my brother that he loved me. I may be jumping to conclusions, but man, my heart is there.

I'm there.

"I'm a horrible person. I thought he ghosted me. I knew his story; he told me. Well, not the recent stuff, but his past, why he left the first time. And I still went straight to thinking I'd been rejected." I slap my hands onto my knees and then cover my face. "I'm so ashamed," I whisper.

"You're ashamed? Man, I think that word better fits me. I'm ashamed. I'm sorry about the other night, Rosie. I was out of line. I was out of my mind in anger," he confesses.

"Yeah, you were pretty intense. Said some really hurtful things." I scuff my tennis shoe on the tile, and it squeaks. I hold it still.

"Yeah, I'm sorry. I was mean. I know that," he admits.

"So why? Why did you make that dig about my bugs? You know, just because I don't like basketball, I'm not a strange girl. I just have different interests. Interests that, mixed with my personality, some find lovable. Even though some of my own family harbors their own resentments," I say, bravely declaring, but at the ground. Not enough courage to look him in the eyes and face him.

"Rosie, you're different than all of us, and we haven't handled that the best over the years. But we love you. I'll do better, I promise. I'm sorry." He pats my back.

"Rosie St. Clair?" A nurse wanders into the waiting room.

"Yes?" My head perks up.

"He's asking for you." She smiles as relief floods my face. I race from my chair and follow the nurse into the hallway.

I'm right on the nurse's heels. "Room 4b," she says.

I pick up my pace. Pushing the door open wide, I burst into the room. My wet shoes squeak on the tile again as I rush to his bedside. I slip and catch myself on his bed.

"I'm sorry, I'm sorry," I say, shaking my head, holding his face

168

in my hands. I'm a mess. Tears stream down my face as he holds my arms, trying to calm me down when he is the one in the hospital bed.

I cry, and he brings my head to his chest, holding me tight.

"I'm okay, I'm okay," he whispers into my hair as my chest heaves in quiet sobs.

"Ma'am, you need to slow down, or you could wind up a patient yourself. Also, be careful with my patient; he is stable now and about to move floors, but let's keep him that way. Kay?" The nurse pokes her head in, scolding me.

I nod into Clarke's chest. "She's got it; thanks, nurse," Clarke tells the woman.

I back up from him and take off Ryder's windbreaker. I pull my legs up onto the hospital bed and snuggle with him. Of course, his body is so big on this thing. I am kind of a koala bear hanging onto him. He runs his fingers through my tangled hair. We stay like that for quite a few moments. Time passes, but the only reason I know that is because the rain clears outside and exposes the afternoon sun beginning to set.

"Clarke, you should have told me about your brother's death. The reason you needed Ryder," I say into his chest and prop myself up onto my elbow.

"Rosie," he whispers, shaking his head, "I didn't want to put you in danger."

"Look here, mister, you play basketball, so you know a thing or two about teammates. I am your teammate in life—that means you have to communicate with me. I'm on your team." I intertwine my fingers with his and place our held hands against his heart.

"You are in danger too, and I deserved to know that. I was so worried. So … so angry. I was wrong, I thought, I thought …"

169

He moves my hair out of my face and brushes his thumb against my cheek.

"I thought you got scared of fake proposing and realized that all of this was a mistake," I put my fears into words. Something I have always internalized in the past. "That I was just a stupid mistake." I move my eyes to his. There is emotion there, not only in mine, but behind his eyes.

"*Rosie.*" His voice is pained as he leans down to kiss me. "You're right—you were wrong. You are not a stupid mistake. You are not *just* Rosie to me. You are an unpredictable breath of fresh air. Like I said the other night, you are the best thing in my life. My biggest blessing. I don't want to lose you." We both nod tearfully. I place my head back on his chest for a little while longer.

***

I follow as the nurse moves him to the recovery ward and watch as Ryder shakes the hands of two police officers set to guard Clarke's room. I mouth, "thank you" to Ryder, and he nods back to me.

A few hours later, I'm watching cartoons with Clarke and feeding him orange Jello. Ryder knocks on the door, and we holler at him to come in.

Clarke nods slowly at him in recognition. He offers his hand to Ryder, and Ryder approaches his bed. He takes his hand in his, and just as I think this will be a normal business handshake, I watch as the two do their bro handshake from high school. Tears fill my eyes, and I nod to myself.

"Hey, I'll be in touch when you get out of here. Take care of yourself and my little sister. And hey, I hope you can make it to Thanksgiving here in the next few weeks. I think you'll remember the address." He smiles, pointing at Clarke while exiting the door.

My face erupts into a smile as I look at Ryder.

You know, even my Morgan Wallen look-alike brother is pretty cool. He may be a hothead, but he's a pretty cool guy. I'm thankful he's taking the case and that he's good at his job. It gives me hope for Clarke. It gives me hope for us. We'll be okay. It'll all be okay.

Chapter 30

Clarke was released after five days in the hospital, his face bruised and a few broken bones that left him injured and out for the rest of the season. Which was definitely a bummer, but it meant more time with me. So how could I really complain? Speaking of more time together, because of Ryder's suggestion, Clarke hired a bodyguard for himself and one for me. We are all hopeful we won't need them forever, but right now, for a season, it is imperative. He needs to be safe, and I need to be safe as Ryder takes this big bad man to trial. We know trials can take a long time, but we are pressing forward, together.

I have a woman bodyguard named Arriana, and his is named Rodney. Honestly, I ship them. What? They are with us twenty-four/seven. They come on dates with us too, so technically they are already dating. I know, I know, but one can't blame me for trying to make the serious situation more lighthearted.

The weather has shifted so much in the past couple weeks. The breeze has turned chilly versus muggy, and the leaves are falling. Thanksgiving dinner at my parents' house is this afternoon, and it will be the first time my parents and Roxy see Clarke again. He's nervous. I'm not, but obviously, that's because of all the redemption I have already seen. If Ryder, my hotheaded and stubborn brother, who may I add, sure knows how to hold a grudge, (like the rest of my family) can forgive Clarke, I'm sure my mom and dad already have. And Roxy? She was so young, what does she really have to forgive? Unless she had a crush on Clarke at age twelve and I had no idea. Arriana and Rodney are coming too. See, I'm serious, *it's a thing. Or will be once I'm done with them.*

***

"You're acting like Mom and Dad have never met your boyfriend before, like you've never brought him home." Roxy leans against the wall in the foyer, talking to me as I pace.

I stare at her. "Well, technically this is the first time they're meeting him as my boyfriend."

"Rosie, the guy spent every waking hour here as a teen. Mom and Dad will be chill."

"What about you?" I scoff.

"Well, that's a different story." She smirks.

"Oh, shut up. You better stay chill, or Arriana will put you in a chokehold."

She rolls her eyes at my absurdity. "Oh, I am so afraid of your bodyguard that is currently cracking pistachios in the kitchen with Dad."

"She could crack you like a pistachio!" I tease Roxy.

"Ope, game time." Roxy points at the door, and I see my man, ascending the stairs. He's sporting a nice white dress shirt and navy slacks. Rodney is steps behind him, sporting all black.

Ding dong.

The doorbell rings, and I act as if he can't see me standing here on the other side of the door. Shamelessly waiting for his arrival. I wipe my hands on my jeans and reach for the door.

"Hey, babe." He leans down and gives me a kiss on the cheek. He holds a bouquet of flowers in his hand for my mom. How sweet.

"Hey." I grin and grab hold of his hand, pulling him in behind me.

"A white shirt to Thanksgiving dinner?" I whisper to him, and he looks down at himself, registering my question.

"Ooh," he ponders aloud.

"Yeah," I chuckle, "I'll get you a big napkin," I say.

"Do they make them that big? I might need a pillowcase." His comment makes me snort out in laughter.

"Oh, Clarke, you're back!" Mom shuffles around the corner and reaches out to hug him.

I take the flowers out of his hands to make room for my mom. She slips her arms around his middle and gives him a big hug.

"We are so glad you are okay. And so super thankful you are back in our lives." She glances up at him and bops his nose with her finger.

My eyes tear up a bit, and I can tell he's trying to keep it together as well.

He finally has a family again.

The front door opens and shuts, and there's an, "Ayye, fam!" at the door. Ryder walks in, in a maroon suit. Always so professional looking. I guess that's why Clarke dressed up. I half expected him to show up in athletic shorts and jersey like they did back in the day.

"Hey, brother." Ryder pats Clarke on the back. "Glad you are here. How you feelin?" he asks him.

"Better and better every day. I even got permission from the doc for a little practice. Though, the team wants me to rest a little longer."

"Hey, I got a good idea, we still got that court out back." Ryder clicks his tongue, pointing to the basketball court in the back yard.

A smile slips onto Clarke's face, and I cross my arms across my chest.

Great.

"I'm in!" Roxy shouts and joins the conversation.

"Okay, you two cripples can be on the same team, and I'll take Rosie," Ryder says.

All of them turn their heads to me.

"Oh, no way." I shake my head. "I am not playing basketball!"

"Oh, come on, sis, I need you!" Ryder begs me.

I feel a trick coming on.

"We'll see," I mutter.

"Well, enough of this, come on in the kitchen and get some appetizers," Dad calls the group of us into the kitchen.

"Pops!" Ryder shakes Dad's hand.

Dad shakes Clarke's hand and smiles. "Good to see you, son!"

My heart erupts with warmth. This is such a sweet ending to the broken and tumultuous story of Clarke's past. Or maybe, I wonder, looking at Clarke across the kitchen.

Maybe it's just the beginning. Our beginning.

***

At the dinner table, our tradition is that everyone goes around and names something they are thankful for.

"I'll go first," Mom says. "I am thankful that Grandpa and Grandma get to have Thanksgiving with their friends at the Senior Center and get to join us later. I am so thankful they have made new friends and settled in so well, considering the obstacles and changes." She smiles and folds her hands in her lap.

"I am thankful that Rosie took over Love in Bloom, and that she took the courageous leap to keep the garden in the family. Really stellar of you, honey." Dad nods towards me.

"Aw, thanks, Dad." I take his words to heart. I haven't always been the recipient of praise, so this feels unusual, yet also wonderful.

"I am thankful for … um," Roxy begins. "I am thankful that I have successfully changed majors from Business Administration to Forensic Accounting. They accepted me into their program. It's hard to get into," she says so matter-of-factly, pretending that we all know this information.

"Roxy!" all of us say in various tones.

"That's great," Mom says, clapping her hands together.

"So proud of you, kiddo." Dad smiles. Now, Dad must have known because there is no way otherwise anyone could drop that kind of bomb at the dinner table. No more business administration? But I mean, I guess it is accounting she is moving into. But did no one else hear that little word "forensic?"

"Rox Box! Awesome, girl!" Ryder nudges her across the table.

"Congrats, sis!" I smile at her; she's over here trying to keep a secret. In actuality, she's probably not trying to do anything other than get through this and then eat. Ha.

"Congratulations, Roxy," Clarke extends his words as well.

"Thank you, thank you all, now it's this muck's turn." She slaps Ryder upside the head, and I choke on the sip of water I'm taking.

"Alright, I uh, you know I've had a lot of great success in

business this year. Uh, but I think what I'm most thankful for this year is having my brother back. It's been too long, man. I've missed ya." He nods to Clarke across the table and raises his glass to him.

Mom raises her glass then, and like dominos, the rest of the family lift theirs.

"To Clarke coming home," Ryder says.

"To Clarke coming home," we all repeat and drink up.

"Great to be home, thank you for inviting me back with such open and loving arms. I'm not sure I deserve it," Clarke says, looking between my mom and dad.

"Nonsense. You belong here," Mom reassures him. I catch him tearing up from the corner of my eye and grab onto his knee under the table.

"Well, I," I speak up. "I have so much to be thankful for, and I hate to be a copycat, but I am definitely most thankful that Clarke came back, and I am thankful that he likes me. Even though I'm the weird bug lady." I smirk and shake my head.

He squeezes my hand under the table as my family erupts into comments such as, "You are *not* the weird girl."

"You are totally kinda weird with those bugs."

"Some of them are cute."

"Oh, Rosie …"

I smile and lean over to Clarke to give him a small kiss on the lips.

He smiles. "Lastly, it's me. I'm thankful for that paparazzi who started that rumor about us at Love in Bloom and started it all. I guess they're not always so bad." His comment makes everyone laugh, and more questions break out—people want to hear the story. Oh boy, well, maybe we will indulge them.

"Okay, okay, let's say prayer and eat!" Dad calms the table, and we bow our heads.

Chapter 31

"Rosie! Come on, girl, you're on my team!" Ryder insists I play basketball with them.

"Fine, but if I am going to play, I'm bringing out the Bluetooth speaker, and we're playing tunes!" I shout.

"Fine!" Ryder shouts back at me.

"Oh no," Roxy comments.

That makes me smile because she knows.

Clarke rolls up his shirt sleeves, buttoning them around his elbows. He claps, encouraging Roxy to throw him the basketball. They start passing it and running drills.

I think.

I'm not totally sure what you call that.

Clarke and Ryder start bobbing their heads to the classic 2000s playlist I put on.

I guess this is really happening.

The food was delicious; everyone is stuffed. So in the name of pie, it was declared that we all must play basketball to gain space in our bellies for pumpkin pie! But how do they know that I didn't leave room?

Ugh, okay, okay, I'm playing.

We huddle up in our respective teams. Ryder slips his suit jacket off and mimics Clarke by rolling up his sleeves as well.

I take off my bulky cardigan, but otherwise am playing in high-waisted jeans and a plain, long-sleeved shirt.

"Here we go!" Ryder claps. "Us versus the cripples!"

I think he is crazy! Two basketball-playing cripples, one being professional, is still better than a wannabe professional player and his incapable at sports sister. If he thinks we have any chance, he is more in his head than I thought.

"Go!" Ryder yells, and they pass the ball back and forth saying, "Check" and then, "Mate." I don't understand that, then Clarke goes flying down the court and passes the ball to Roxy. She dribbles it and does a layup.

"Woo!" Clarke howls and slaps Roxy's hand.

Man, she can get around pretty good on her foot now—not perfect, but she's doing better. Though, and we didn't ask inside at dinner, but my big question with her getting accepted into this hard program is if she is giving up college ball.

"Rosie, where is your head? Get in the game, girl," Ryder hollers at me, waving his arm so I can pass it to him.

"Oh!" I yell and then do exactly that—pass it to him. Although it gets stolen midair by Roxy and taken to the basket.

"Hey, come on! You're not going to take any pity on me at all?" I shout and plead with my hands.

She just shakes her head, smirking. Giving Clarke another high-five.

Ryder agrees, "Hey, yeah, I don't think that's fair."

"Hey, you picked the teams, man!" Roxy yells at him.

"Okay, time out!" Ryder shouts and brings me in to chat.

"We're not trading players now!" Roxy shouts at him.

"For the record, I wouldn't mind." Clarke grins, checking me out.

Roxy smacks him in the arm. "No."

He laughs and gives me an air kiss.

That gives me an idea, and I pull Ryder closer to me to whisper in his ear.

At first, he gives me some grief over my idea and pushes back.

So we run another play.

After that one fails, he gives me the green light on my plan.

I bounce the ball to Clarke. "Check," and he replies, "Mate."

I start running and dribbling the ball as best as I can. Ryder stands under the basket, and Clarke stands in front of me, blocking my attempts to deliver the ball to Ryder. I take the ball into one hand and my other reaches around Clarke's neck. I pull on him to collide our lips together. Caught up in the moment, Clarke slips his hands around my waist, kissing me fully. I toss the ball aimlessly toward Ryder and wrap my arms around Clarke's neck.

"Oh, yuck," Roxy says dryly. "There's no kissing in basketball!" Roxy shouts at me and Ryder. She prefers rules to be followed. "Clarke, come on, man, be strong!" Roxy urges him.

"Sorry, you have no idea what your sister does to me." He laughs, a big grin on his face.

"Okay, yeah, you're right, Rox! Gross, guys, break it up!" Ryder calls over to us as Clarke spins me in a circle on the court.

"I don't know, I think I'm being ejected! Don't you hear them calling my name?" he teases the others.

"I agree! I hear it too!" I giggle.

"Oh, get a room, you two!" Roxy rolls her eyes.

He sets me down and holds my hand.

"We're going on a walk," Clarke shouts to my siblings.

"Fine, come on, Rox, let's play H-O-R-S-E." Ryder pats her shoulder, getting all excited. Roxy just looks annoyed.

Poor Roxy.

"We'll meet you guys later for pie and football!" Clarke shouts to them one more time.

"To watch, right? I'm done with sports today," I tell him, hanging on his arm.

"Is kissing considered a sport?" He leans down, teasing me.

"Not in my book," I whisper, giving him an Eskimo kiss.

"Oh, good." He presses his lips to mine again.

As we head out on our walk around the neighborhood, our bodyguards trail just a bit behind us. Yes, this is my shameless idea to get the two of them together. As I eye them to try and figure out if they're holding hands yet, my hand brushes against my bag.

That reminds me! I pull my crossbody bag to the front of me. As we approach the third stop sign on our route around my parents' neighborhood, I slow to a stop.

"What's up?" Clarke asks me.

I pull an envelope out of my bag and flash it before his eyes.

"I got this in the mail." I shrug, bracing myself.

"Rosalie St. Clair," he reads. "Sounds official. It's from the Research Institute. Open it." He pokes my side and smiles.

He urges me to open the envelope, so I nod, blushing. I'm nervous.

I open the envelope, careful to not get a paper cut. The letter opens in front of me, and my eyes instantly catch on the word,

"Congratulations!"

"Oh my goodness! Oh my goodness!" I repeat, placing one hand up to cover my mouth.

"What? What is it?" Clarke appears fully intrigued.

"A donor toured the lab early in the morning, that night I slept there. I … I … guess I didn't see him because I was asleep. He told the Institute that he wanted to know the project I was working on because he was inspired by my dedication. To be there all night working in the lab alone." I glance up at Clarke in shock. Who knew there would be another positive out of that situation?

"He is donating my full portion to the Spongy Moth research project." I blink, tears filling my eyes.

"Rosie, that's incredible. I'm so proud of you for never giving up on your dreams." Clarke moves his palm to my cheek and dips his forehead into mine.

"This means that my grandparents will get what they need from the rose garden. I will even have what I need to continue to invest in it for years to come." I close my eyes and breathe in my blessings.

The donation. My critters. The roses. My family. And *my man.*

What a happy Thanksgiving indeed.

***

The Dallas Cowboys are able to pull out a win, and my brother is excited as he bet my dad twenty dollars that they would win. The sun has set outside, and I spy that large oak out back. I shift in Clarke's arms on the sofa. Everyone is starting to fix little appetizer plates once more. Except for us. I see an opportunity, and I want him to come too.

I press my mouth against his ear. "Follow me."

I pull my cardigan back on and remove the blanket from my legs. He sets the cable knit blanket beside him on the couch and stands, reaching out to hold my hand.

"We'll be right back," I tell my family (and bodyguards), as we exit through the back patio door.

I hear chatter as we make our way outside, "Where do you think they're going?" and a big disgruntled noise from Roxy, "Ugh, the tree."

I giggle, pulling him close behind me.

"Man, it's chilly out here. What a stark contrast from that hot night in May," he says.

"Hey," I reach up and touch his face, "enough of that talk. We are new people now."

He smiles and looks up at the moonlight. "Yeah, you're right." He nods.

"Not to mention, you're like five feet taller now too." He busts into laughter.

"Five whole feet, huh?" he teases me, backing up from me for a moment, taking in the backyard.

We stand there for a moment, and even though I just said it's different, for a moment, I close my eyes, picturing us back there that night.

As I open my eyes, it's as if he is acting it out as well. He walks closer to me, reaching out his hands, and slowly envelopes mine in his.

This time though, I notice that his expression isn't sad, it isn't confused. It's one of peace and happiness.

"Rosalie," he whispers to me, and my heart rate picks up just like it did that night long ago. I remember again, a boy had never held my hands. A boy had never looked at me so longingly while they said my name. And even though I didn't

184

know it then, Clarke would still be the only boy who ever held my hands, ever longingly said my name.

My eyes look between him and the moon, and the cold breeze blows my blonde hair into my eyes. He reaches out his hand and moves my hair back. The way his hand brushes up against my cheek … he is so gentle, such a kind man.

He leans in a bit, and I know where this ends. The first time, of course, it ended with goodbye between two people destined to fall in love. But this time, it continues. With a beautiful kiss shared between two people … two people who, well …

"Clarke, I love you." My eyes jump across his face as a smile stretches across it.

"I love you too, Rosie. I love you too." He reaches down, this time capturing my lips with his own.

The ending and beginning of a beautiful story.

The story of us.

***

Join me for Book 2 in the Beyond the Buzzer Series.
It's Roxy St. Clair's story.
Coming 2025.

About the Author

Hi!

My pen name is Hattie Wade. I am a Christian Author who lives in the Midwest! I write Christian Romance, Clean Romance and Children's Mystery Novels. I started writing books in 2020 and currently have six books published. In my free time you can find me spending time with family and friends, antiquing, drinking sparkling water, and listening to music on my record player.

You can connect with me on:

🌐 https://www.authorhattiewade.weebly.com

🔗 https://www.instagram.com/authorhattiewade

Also by Hattie Wade

HE REDEEMS, A CHRISTIAN ROMANCE SERIES:
  Run to Him (2022)
  Rely on Him (2023)
  Rest in Him (2023)

COWBOY NOVELLA SERIES:
  Her Washed-Up Cowboy (2023)
  Her Maybe Sorta Kinda Cowboy (Writing In Progress)

THE PLUM CREEK DETECTIVE GIRLS SERIES:
  The Case Of The Gentle Giant (2024)
  The Case Of The Tilted Time Capsule (Writing In Progress)

BEYOND THE BUZZER, A BASKETBALL ROMANCE SERIES:
  Rebounds & Roses (2024)
  Title To Be Determined (Writing In Progress)
  Hoops & Hearts (Writing In Progress)

STAND ALONE CHRISTIAN ROMANCE:
  A Vow Of Hope (Writing In Progress)

Made in the USA
Columbia, SC
11 November 2024

45936621R00119